A GAME OF SURVIVAL HORROR

ASH BARKER

OSPREY
GAMES

OSPREY GAMES

Bloomsbury Publishing Plc

Kemp House, Chawley Park, Cumnor Hill, Oxford OX2 9PH, UK

1385 Broadway, 5th Floor, New York, NY 10018, USA

Email: info@ospreygames.co.uk

www.ospreygames.co.uk

OSPREY GAMES is a trademark of Osprey Publishing, a division of
Bloomsbury Publishing Plc

First published in Great Britain in 2018

ISBN: HB 978 1 4728 2669 5
eBook 978 1 4728 2670 1
ePDF 978 1 4728 2671 8
XML 978 1 4728 2672 5

Typeset in Adobe Garamond Pro, Alternate Gothic No 2, and Peixe Frito
Originated by PDQ Digital Media Solutions, Bungay, UK
Printed and bound in India by Replika Press Private Ltd.

20 21 22 23 24   10 9 8 7 6 5 4 3

The Woodland Trust
Osprey Publishing supports the Woodland Trust, the UK's leading woodland
conservation charity.

www.ospreygames.co.uk
To find out more about our authors and books visit our website. Here you will find
extracts, author interviews, details of forthcoming events and the option to sign-up
for our newsletter.

CONTENTS

FOREWORD

This will be the second time I've written a foreword for this game. The first time was in 2009 when I drafted its original incarnation. I guess, technically, that makes this the Second Edition of *Last Days*. The first time it has ever been published, but hardly the first time it has ever been played.

It's funny how things turn out.

As a kid, my imagination was captured by the old zombie movies of the 60s and 70s. Romero's nightmare vision and social commentary stuck with me as an adolescent, through my teens and into my twenties, and I voraciously soaked up the genre in all its forms. While in hindsight it seems only logical that this is the first game I ever put to print, it was not an interest that crossed into my miniature wargaming hobby until much later.

The first version of *Last Days* was conceived during a period in which I was traveling constantly for work. It was before I married or had kids and I was almost always on the move. My hobby had become consumed by work and I was collecting bits and pieces of models from all over for a change of pace. It just happened that there was a small explosion of companies putting out random zombie apocalypse themed models at the time and I was collecting them as they came out. I found myself with quite a collection of themed miniatures. They made me happy because I had painted them just because I liked them, not because I was intending for them to be used in any specific game.

It struck me during a long drive between meetings that this collection could easily be used in a game. I was inspired and my laptop would be cracked open each night in my hotel and another section was completed before I would pass out and get back on the road the next day.

The result was a game that my friends and I played quite a bit. Most recently the original version was played with and recorded on my YouTube channel. These new players seemed to quite enjoy it.

The problem was I didn't enjoy it. Not nearly as much as I remembered.

When the reality that it was going to be published finally sank in, I looked

at the original version of the game. Really looked at it. I needed to figure out what it was missing.

Assessing my creation, I reflected on all the games I'd played between first drafting it and now. A lot had happened. I'd left my job and returned home to Canada. I'd had two wonderfully mad children and found a niche for myself sharing my hobby on the internet in a moderately successful home business. I'd also played over a thousand games of all types in the space of three years. Think about that. It's almost a game a day.

What was my game missing? I love small-scale skirmish games. I'd played a lot of really great, new games in the recent years since writing my own. Far more than I'd played previously in my life.

Finally it dawned on me, it didn't make me feel any particular way. It didn't make me feel excited, or nervous, or involved. I didn't feel particularly invested either. It was cleanly written and competently structured but as I pored over it, I felt like it didn't have a soul.

That did it. I had a place to jump off. I wanted my game to have a soul. With that in mind I combed over the games I had really loved. What did they have in common? What things made me feel certain ways while I was playing it?

Digging deep I was able to come up with three things. I've given them names because it helps me keep track of them in the game. They're like touchstones I've used while doing a draft. When designing an element did it accomplish one of these things? A metric I could measure components with.

Those three things I called Memorable Moments, Crackerjacks, and Ever-Afters.

Memorable Moments contained all the surprises that games can throw at you. One of the keystones of skirmish gaming is that they're like playing a pen and paper RPG in a lot of ways, but without a Game Master. The GM is usually the one that pulls the rug out or generates moments of surprise when the narrative tilts or an encounter changes dramatically for some reason. Good skirmish games include elements that create this experience for the players. Loathed in competitive wargaming, these are the things that separate skirmish games from strategy games. The left turn, the curveball event, the pit trap, or looming monster in the dark are all things that create Memorable Moments. The player should never feel like a game will be the same twice because there's always the chance that the progressive generation of events will make it a whole new challenge.

Crackerjacks are the prize at the bottom of the box. That feeling of anticipation when you don't know what they are or accomplishment when the thing you get is really cool is something that can hook a player on a skirmish game. You want to be surprised, delighted, and sometimes even the most bungled game can become eminently satisfying because the lone survivor limped away with a truly cool reward. That sense of mystery and surprise can be generated in lots of ways in skirmish games. It has been harnessed in other markets by something as simple as making a product that you open for a random award. Trillions of discarded foil packages for competitive card games prove this idea is one that is a staple of games in general.

Ever-Afters are the threads that tie games together. A great skirmish game doesn't just tell the events of the game itself but also keeps the story going afterwards. What happened to that model after he was taken out? What went on between the games themselves? Players will naturally inject that stuff themselves if they're creative. A great game will give players either nudges or tasks to help weave the story long after the scenery has been tidied up. It should result in lots of laughing talks after the club has all gone home as to what the next game might mean or who should really be playing who next week as it makes sense to the developing plot-line. Just like great books and movies always leave the player with just enough to keep the brain working after the main plot is done, a good game can contain elements to do the same.

So armed with these weapons and a laptop, I set off to re-write *Last Days* and apply all that I'd reflected on, to craft something that was my take on these ideas. I wanted players to get a game that felt like their little toy soldiers really were living in the *Last Days* of the human race, surrounded by the living dead. This book is the result.

LAST DAYS
ZOMBIE APOCALYPSE

Zombies. Biters. Walkers. No one knows what caused the epidemic that ended civilization. No one knows where it started. Organized resistance has broken down and governments and the military are just rumors passed from survivor to survivor around campfires or huddled in barricaded basements.

The world of *Last Days* is a nightmare near-future infested with the living dead. Animated corpses that seem driven by a feral instinct to feed. Uncoordinated and dangerous, primarily in large groups, they nevertheless overthrew mankind in a matter of weeks. At first they were just a story on the news. Something happening in the cities or far across the country. Then they were in your town. Your neighborhood. At your door.

The game lets you take control of the story of a group of survivors trying to make it just one more day in the zombie apocalypse.

The threats they face are many. The living dead are an omnipresent issue. They have changed everything and will inform decisions from the mundane to the critical, day-by-day.

GENERAL GAME CONCEPTS

Last Days is a tabletop strategy game and as such it is played with miniatures. All of the Characters listed later in this book are man-sized creatures (or appropriately scaled animals) in the 28 to 32mm range. As such they should be mounted on 25-30mm bases of any shape you like (round, square, or hex.... who cares?). This will allow your models to fit in the dense scenery we recommend later on when we discuss setting up the table. It is important that before we go any further we define five conventions that will be used throughout *Last Days*. These conventions are the: Roll-Off, Tests, Measurement, Model's Eye View, and Contact.

ROLL-OFF

The Roll-Off is a simple mechanism for seeing who goes first. Both player roll a six-sided die, re-rolling ties. Whoever rolls higher has the won the Roll-Off.

TESTS

Tests are when a Character needs to achieve something using one of its characteristics. Any Test will have a number and a characteristic associated with it (Intelligence/8). A Character rolls a die (1D6) and adds their characteristic. If this sum equals or exceeds the Test number then they have succeeded. If the sum is less, they have failed. Sometimes Tests can be opposed. In an Opposed Test two Characters will roll a die (1D6) and add their relative characteristic. This is most commonly done in Close Quarters Combat or when opposing Horror and Courage. The Character with the higher sum will be the victor. Unless specifically noted otherwise for a Test, ties are considered a success for the person with the higher characteristic. If this is still a draw, it goes to the Character that did not initiate the Test (the defender).

MEASUREMENT

All Measurements in a game of *Last Days* are in inches and should be from closest base edge to base edge. For instance, when a model moves you must measure the distance it goes from the front of the base to the front of the base, not the front to the back! Any distance can be pre-measured, at any time, in games of *Last Days*.

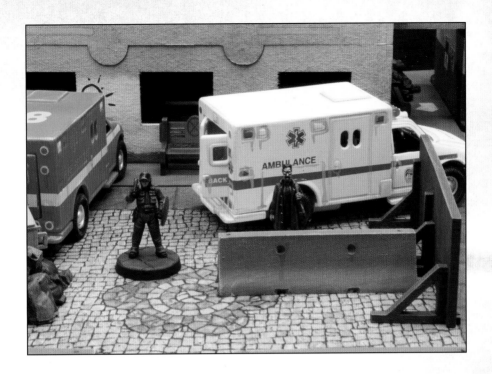

CONTACT

Contact is when two models from opposing Groups (or a zombie) have moved towards each other to the point where their bases are now touching. This is typically done to initiate Close Quarters Combat. If a model does not have enough Action Points to get into Contact then it may not fight in Close Quarters Combat.

MODEL'S EYE VIEW

Where a model can see is referred to as the Model's Eye View. Often during a game it may become necessary to get down near the table to get a look at what your model can see. The basic convention here is that if at least one quarter of a model's body is visible (or any part of its base) from the head of the model wishing to attack, then the attack can be made. This will be talked about more later-on and is referred to as having Line of Sight. Three possibilities exist: Models can either in they open, in cover (obscured by anything between them and the shooter), or they are out of Line of Sight.

These rules are intentionally uncomplicated. The most commonly disputed one will always be Line of Sight. In this case just Roll-Off to see who is in the right… or just stop trying to win so badly and go back to having fun!

CHARACTERISTICS

Characters in games of *Last Days* have eight different characteristics that define their abilities, strengths, and weaknesses during the game. Except for Action Points, characteristics can range from zero to six. A characteristic of zero obviously represents someone with no aptitude in a certain area at all, whereas a six would be someone highly skilled in that area.

All Character types have a name by a dash and then a second word. The second word is that Character's Keyword. Keywords become important when you begin gathering your group. All models will have at least one Keyword, sometimes more.

ACTION POINTS [AP]

Action Points are used by characters to get around the battlefield. They can also be spent to do things like reloading firearms, climbing a wall, or other physical tasks that do not have their own phase. Each Action Point a model has can be used to move an inch, open or bar a door, etc. As you can see from the above examples, a human survivor can move much further than a shambling corpse. Action Points are the only characteristic which can go higher than six.

CLOSE QUARTERS COMBAT [CQC]

A model's Close Quarter Combat characteristic represents its ability to fight with hand to hand weapons or even its bare hands, in the case of the living dead. The undead and living are fairly evenly matched in close combat. Zombies make up for their lack of skill with pure savagery!

FIREARMS [FA]

The Firearms characteristic represents a models ability to operate and fire ranged weapons (both conventional and otherwise). Obviously, the undead cannot operate these weapons (hence the 0 characteristic), while the average human survivor has a respectable chance of hitting their intended target with a weapon.

STRENGTH [S]

The Strength characteristic represents a model's physical capability to inflict damage or carry a heavy load. You can see in the above examples that both the human survivor and the zombie have the same strength (they are after all generally the same, simply in different stages of decomposition).

ENDURANCE (E)

Endurance represents a models toughness, ability to deal with pain and resistance to damage. You will notice that the human survivor has a respectable Endurance of three, while the Zombie doesn't even have an Endurance characteristic at all. The reason for this is obvious, they don't need one! This will all be explained under the Zombies section later, but the most important thing to remember is to Shoot them in the head! (see page 61).

DAMAGE CAPACITY (DC)

The Damage Capacity characteristic is representative of a models ability to operate while injured. The higher the number, the more times a model can take damage before they succumb to their injuries and pass out or expire.

COURAGE/HORROR (C/H)

Courage and Horror are opposed characteristics and represent a models ability to cope with, or cause, fear and terror. The human survivor has a Courage characteristic, as he will be forced to deal with horrifying situations on pretty much a day-to-day basis. The zombie has a Horror characteristic as, obviously, it isn't a pretty sight! Being attacked almost constantly by these ghouls is stressful in the middle of a fight, so the higher a model's Courage the better.

INTELLIGENCE (I)

The Intelligence characteristic represents a model's capacity for dealing with complex problems under stress. From something as simple as getting into a locked door to hotwiring a getaway vehicle, this stat will be used to deal with problems during the game that can't be solved with gnashing teeth or spraying bullets. The human survivor has a basic intelligence of three, while the zombie has an intelligence of zero. Locked doors can be very handy in keeping the undead at bay!

An example Survivor and Zombie profile is shown below.

SURVIVOR – NEUTRAL

AP	CQC	FA	S	E	DC	C	I
6	3	3	3	3	3	3	3

ZOMBIE – REVENANT

AP	CQC	FA	S	E	DC	H	I
5	3	0	3	*	1	3	0

PREPARING TO PLAY

In the beginning you won't need much to play *Last Days*. As you progress – should you find yourself enjoying it – you might devote some time to designing custom terrain pieces. You might build encampments that represent where your Group hides and survives the night, and even converting alternate models to represent different injuries or load-outs your characters develop as they fight to survive a Campaign.

To get started however you simply need:

- Some appropriate models to represent your Groups.
- 20 zombie models.
- A handful of six sided dice.
- Measuring devices in inches.
- Some printed cards for your Characters to track their stats and various in game effects. You can photocopy them from the back of the book. Putting them in clear plastic sleeves and using a dry-wipe marker will make life even easier.
- A 3'x3' gaming surface. You can play with larger or smaller areas but the game is designed to be fairly intimate and dialled in closely to the action. This area works best.
- Appropriate model terrain to represent your desired location during the zombie apocalypse, whether it's rural Georgia or the mean streets of Chicago.

The rest of this book is laid out in the order most of you will approach trying a new miniature game; from assembling what you need to play to playing the game itself. The first thing we'll concern ourselves with is bringing together your group of survivors under the leadership of a powerful figure, which in game terms, we simply always refer to as 'The Leader'.

GATHERING YOUR GROUP

The zombie apocalypse is often a rogue's gallery of heroes and villains. Stress and instinct in desperate survival situations can bring out both the best and the worst in people. What does that mean for **your** Group? How have they chosen to survive? What's brought them together?

Give this a little thought because you'll enjoy your games more if you've got some inkling of a backstory for everyone in your merry little band. Or don't. Your call. You'll certainly laugh more when Larry the Flight Attendant goes down swinging a bat having just killed twenty zombies screaming, 'NOW BOARDING ZONE TWO' than if he's just some random figure with a club. Trust me.

Every Group in the zombie apocalypse has one thing in common, a strong personality that has pulled them together and helped them survive. This person is what will set the tone and theme for your Group. Pick one that you think fits the theme you have in mind or the models you really like.

Your initial budget for recruiting a Group is 100 Scavenge Points. The cost of your Leader comes from this same pool. Scavenge Points are a currency that will be used later on to augment your refuge and equip newly discovered Characters, so it's okay to bank any Scavenge Points leftover after gathering your initial Group.

CHOOSING A LEADER

Your Leader will set the tone for your entire Group. His priorities and alignment will dictate with who he surrounds himself and the shape of the Group as a whole. In addition to the normal characteristics, each Leader presented here will have a chart of Group preferences. When you create the rest of the Group, this will dictate how many individuals of differing philosophies he might tolerate or even what types of equipment your group can use. Other leader types are planned for the future but here are the three classic archetypes for those that find themselves in the position of leading a Group in *Last Days*. Your Group may only ever contain a single Leader.

THE EVERYDAY HERO – SELFLESS

12 Scavenge Points

Whether simply a person of unusual character, an A-type personality or a grocery store clerk. The Everyday Hero is someone you can rely on to keep things groovy when things go all zombie apocalypse. He's taken charge of this group of survivors and will do whatever it takes to keep them safe.

AP	CQC	FA	S	E	DC	C	I
6	4	3	3	3	3	4	3

Special Rules	Leader
Skills Available	Leader, Firearms, CQC, Academic
Group Preferences	None

THE MERCILESS THUG – SELFISH

15 Scavenge Points

When it falls apart some people are transformed. Whoever this person was, he now rules with an iron fist. He is the toughest, most brutal member of the Group and rewards disloyalty by leaving his enemies naked on the streets, tied up for the living dead. His group is his way of surviving and he'll spend their lives for the sake of his own without a second thought.

AP	CQC	FA	S	E	DC	C	I
6	4	3	4	3	3	3	3

Special Rules	Leader
Skills Available	Leader, Firearms, CQC, Athletic
Group Preferences	A Group led by this character may increase the number of Neutral models it may hire to 75% of the total group number but may not hire a Good Samaritan, Cop, SWAT, or Kid.

THE PROFESSIONAL – TRAINED

18 Scavenge Points

The Professional is respected by his Group and (sometimes regardless of background or former ranks) has risen to keep this elite group together through the fall of civilization. He is, however, attached to the old world and his training makes it hard for him and his group to adapt to new ways of survival.

AP	CQC	FA	S	E	DC	C	I
6	4	4	3	3	3	4	3

Special Rules	Leader
Skills Available	Leader, Firearms, CQC, Athletic, Academic
Group Preferences	A Group led by this character may only use equipment marked with a '*' (see pages 30 and 74–78). The Professional frowns on non-traditional weapons or tactics and will never send anyone out armed in a way he does not consider 'sensible'. Likewise, if they find equipment not marked with an '*' during the game they may not choose to use it while this character is the Leader, but it may be put in the group Stash.

Your Leader may be equipped with weapons and items using the same rules as the remainder of your Group. This will be detailed later on. Character cards are available at the back of this book to photocopy and print out (see page 110). Give your Leader a name and note down his details before you move on to the next section.

DESIGN NOTE

If this is your first time playing *Last Days* then you're likely wondering how you will go about collecting forces to play. The simplest suggestion is that you begin by finding models you like and that suit your setting. Let the models dictate who leads your group by finding one that you really like and which is suitably impressive. Look through the cast of Characters that can join your Group and try to match them up by how they look and the theme that Character type projects. You will get to playing the game much more quickly if you just let the model's obvious equipment make your choices early on instead of worrying about absorbing all the rules up front or what is 'best' in game terms.

CHOOSING A REFUGE

How a Group survives the night surrounded by hungry corpses, how big it can be, and even how many members it can contain is dictated by one thing in *Last Days*; it's Refuge. Where do they bar the windows and doors? What keeps the zombies out? How many beds are there? These are all real questions to ask yourself when you are choosing a Refuge. Your Group has six initial options for Refuges in *Last Days*. You can only pick one, but you may at some point be forced out of it and forced to pick another!

Every Refuge comes with three key features. The first and most important is the Maximum Group Size. People have to physically fit inside a space they and problems develop rapidly with too many people in too few beds over time. It is possible to increase the maximum Group size of a Refuge, but when you're initially creating a Group this could dictate how many characters your Group can start with.

The next feature is how much Empty Space is inside the building your Group is fortifying. This gives your Group the ability to work on and enhance a Refuge to better help them survive each night and scavenge during the day. Between games your Characters can be given jobs, such as building new Perks into a Refuge. For now simply consider that the more spaces a Refuge has, the more flexible it is for your Group in the future.

Each Refuge has its own built-in Perks. Groups of survivors will initially flee to certain locations because they offer some advantage the Group thinks will be important in the future. Built-in Perks can never be removed, like the ones you might build yourself later on, as they're typically part of the structure or nature of the location itself, so bear that in mind when you select your starting place of hiding. These Perks do not take up any of the Empty Space.

Refuge Type	Max. Group Size	Empty Spaces	Built-In Perks
The Farm House	8	6	Fenced-Off Garden
The Mall	12	8	Store Room
The Gun Shop	6	3	Armoury, Fortified Windows, Reinforced Doors
The Police Station	8	2	Escape Vehicle, Radio Room
The Church	8	2	Solid Structure, Watch Tower
The Prison	10	3	Fences, Infirmary

Handy, printable cards are provided to keep track of your Refuge at the end of this book. You'll only ever have a single Refuge at any given time, so simply print off one and fill in the details of the one you have selected. It can be useful to cross out all but the available Empty Spaces so you'll know how many you have in the future as well as highlighting your built-in Perk in some way so you don't try to demolish it later.

ASSEMBLING YOUR CHARACTERS

Now that your Leader and Refuge have been chosen, it is time to assemble the remainder of your Group. The world is full of people with a variety of backgrounds and skills. If someone has survived this long during the collapse of civilization then they are either committed, lucky, or crazy. Possibly all three.

Who makes up you group will be to a large degree determined by your leader. Characters are divided by their Keywords. For the bulk of your group this will be the thing they have in common. Leaders tend to attract folks aligned to the same beliefs. They may tolerate some members who have other points of view but these will be outliers, often slightly outcast, and barely tolerated by the rest of the Group.

When recruiting your Characters you must abide by the following conditions:

- You may recruit any number of Characters with the **same** Keyword as your Leader.
- Up to 50% of the Characters in your Group may have the Neutral Keyword. These characters are morally flexible and tend to emulate the behaviors of the Leader themselves.
- Only 25% or less of the models in your Group may have a **different** Keyword than your Leader. Their opposing viewpoints cause arguments and dissension amongst the group and undermine the Leader's decisions so they only tolerate a bare minimum of them.

Remember you must pay for your Characters, Leader, and their equipment from your 100 Scavenge Point budget, so consider what each will be carrying. They may find different and better equipment later on, but they will have to earn it by scavenging it in games! Recruitment is the only time you can pick and choose how a Character is armed, but you can swap and exchange items later on.

Some Characters will come with built in skills. Note these down on their Character cards when you create them. They will also each have certain skill types available to them as they learn and progress. Note which of these are available in the notes section of the card.

Write down the details of each Character on a card. These are available at the back of the book to Photocopy and each Character should have one.

CHARACTER TYPES

COP - TRAINED

9 Scavenge Points

Cops can come from any number of different areas: local police, sheriffs, and even private security. They typically have worked together for some time and respect the decisions made by their leader.

AP	CQC	FA	S	E	DC	C	I
6	3	4	3	3	3	3	3
Special Rules	None						
Skills Available	Firearms, Academic						

CRONY - SELFISH

3 Scavenge Points

The Crony helps sell the invincible image of the leader. To survive, they have attached themselves to the strong. The leader's fondness for them keeps them protected fiercely from harm and they are often a rallying point for the Group.

AP	CQC	FA	S	E	DC	C	I
5	2	2	3	3	3	2	2
Special Rules	Inspirational Presence						
Skills Available	Academic						

DOG - NEUTRAL

9 Scavenge Points

How this furry fellow has lived this long is beyond you, but so long as you're feeding him, he just won't stop following you around!

AP	CQC	FA	S	E	DC	C	I
8	4	0	3	3	3	4	1
Special Rules	Noisy 1, Crowd Control, Animal						
Skills Available	None						

FIREFIGHTER - SELFLESS

12 Scavenge Points

Well used to putting themselves in harms-way and more physically adept than the average person, Firefighters often find themselves at the head of a group, kicking in doors and hauling the vital supplies back to the Refuge.

AP	CQC	FA	S	E	DC	C	I
8	3	3	3	3	3	4	3

Special Rules	Heavy Lifter, Entry Man
Skills Available	CQC, Athletic

GANG MEMBER - SELFISH

6 Scavenge Points

Gang members can come from just about anywhere, much like the survivors of other groups. What sets them apart is that they deem their own survival more important than any morals they may have had before the plague hit.

AP	CQC	FA	S	E	DC	C	I
6	3	3	3	3	3	2	2

Special Rules	None
Skills Available	CQC, Firearms

GOOD SAMARITAN - SELFLESS

9 Scavenge Points

This could be the local pastor, a guidance councillor, the kid that volunteers at a soup kitchen, or your local park ranger. The important thing is that they will put others first and try to help other Group members when things start to go wrong.

AP	CQC	FA	S	E	DC	C	I
6	3	3	3	3	3	3	3

Special Rules	Inspirational Presence
Skills Available	CQC, Academic

GOON – 5ELFI5H

9 Scavenge Points

Goons aren't the smartest people on earth but they're tough as hell and know that so long as they're loyal dogs, the leader will cut them in on the best loot.

AP	CQC	FA	S	E	DC	C	I
5	4	3	3	4	3	2	2

Special Rules	None
Skills Available	CQC, Athletic

KID – NEUTRAL

3 Scavenge Points

He won't really talk about anything before you found him but the kid is smart and clearly lucky. He also provides focus to the rest of the group; no one wants to see him get hurt.

AP	CQC	FA	S	E	DC	C	I
6	2	0	2	2	2	3	3

Special Rules	Inspirational Presence
Skills Available	Pick any one skill type when you create the Character, except Leader

RESCUE WORKER – SELFLESS

9 Scavenge Points

A Rescue Worker could be a paramedic, nurse, or even just a swim instructor. The important thing is that they can patch you up with whatever's handy when you're hurt, and know enough to stave off infection and death.

AP	CQC	FA	S	E	DC	C	I
6	3	3	3	3	3	3	3

Special Rules	First Aid Training
Skills Available	Academic, Athletic

SARGE – TRAINED

21 Scavenge Points

Usually second in command of the Group, Sarge is the one who the men turn to when the going gets tough. He is the heart of the Group, where the Leader is the brains.

AP	CQC	FA	S	E	DC	C	I
6	4	4	3	4	3	4	3

Special Rules	Tactical Acumen
Skills Available	Athletic, CQC, Firearms, Leader

SOLDIER – TRAINED

12 Scavenge Points

Soldiers that have seen too much as the world around them fell. Those that have survived have the kind of thousand-yard stare that unsettles everyone around them.

AP	CQC	FA	S	E	DC	C	I
6	3	4	3	3	3	4	3

Special Rules	None
Skills Available	Athletic, CQC, Firearms, Academic

SURVIVALIST - SELFISH

18 Scavenge Points

He's always a little edgy looking and he never stops cleaning his guns… but the Survivalist can get you into pretty much every stash of canned goods left on the planet. He's not bad when the bullets start flying either.

AP	CQC	FA	S	E	DC	C	I
6	4	3	3	3	3	3	3
Special Rules	Scavenger, Gunsmith (choose the weapon type when you create the character)						
Skills Available	CQC, Firearms						

SURVIVOR - NEUTRAL

6 Scavenge Points

Survivors can be anyone: truck drivers, video-store employees, or even stockbrokers. They're all equal once society has broken down and the lights go dark.

AP	CQC	FA	S	E	DC	C	I
6	3	3	3	3	3	3	3
Special Rules	None						
Skills Available	Pick any two skill types except Leader when you create the Character						

SWAT - TRAINED

12 Scavenge Points

These law enforcement agents have been specially trained to deal with whatever normal police can't handle; hostage situations, search and rescue, nothing is beyond their training, except the living dead.

AP	CQC	FA	S	E	DC	C	I
6	4	4	3	3	3	3	3

Special Rules	Entry Man
Skills Available	Athletic, CQC, Firearms, Academic

TOUGH GUY - NEUTRAL

9 Scavenge Points

Football stars, bouncers, or maybe even drug-dealers. Tough Guys can come in handy when a corpse is trying to chew your leg off.

AP	CQC	FA	S	E	DC	C	I
6	4	3	3	3	3	3	3

Special Rules	None
Skills Available	Athletic and one other skill type chosen when you create the Character

STARTING EQUIPMENT OPTIONS

Each Character in your group **must** start with at least one weapon with which to defend themselves from hostile groups and the living dead. They may carry up to two Firearms and two Close Quarter Combat weapons (CQC). When you recruit a new character it is the **only** time you may freely pick weapons and equipment for them. You may do this when you first create your Group and when you attempt to recruit new Group members between games. Don't forget to arm your Leader as well!

Each weapon has two important things to bear in mind, these are its cost in Scavenge Points and its Rarity. Even with doors unlocked and most of the populace killed, there simply aren't enough of certain weapons for them to show up more than occasionally when a new character joins the Group. If there is a '-' instead of a number, the weapon is common and any number of models may be armed with it. You may of course find more weapons later that takes you over the rarity number, but you may not purchase them for new Characters unless that number drops.

The only exception to this is if your Group is led by a Trained Leader. If that is the case any weapon marked with a '*' may have its rarity changed to '-', representing that Leader's better knowledge and access to those types of weapons.

Remember that a group whose Leader has the Trained Keyword will only be able to select weapons and equipment marked with an '*'.

Characters may also begin the campaign with some miscellaneous equipment. This is noted on their Character card when it is purchased.

Once you have spent your initial 100 Scavenge Points recruiting and equipping your Leader, Group, and have moved into a Refuge, it's time to set up your first game!

EQUIPMENT TABLE			
Firearms			
Weapon Name	Type	Rarity	Scavenge Cost
Revolver*	Pistol	-	2
Semi-Automatic*	Pistol	-	3
Magnum*	Pistol	-	3
Sawed-Off or Breach Loading Shotgun	Shotgun	-	3
Pump-Action Shotgun *	Shotgun	-	5
Surplus SMG	SMG	2	4
Military SMG *	SMG	1	6
Hunting Rifle	Rifle	-	4
High-Power Rifle *	Rifle	1	7
Surplus Assault Rifle	Rifle	2	6
Military Assault Rifle *	Rifle	1	8
Squad Automatic Weapon *	Heavy	1	10
Hunting Bow	Sporting	-	3
Hunting Crossbow	Sporting	2	4
Close Quarters Combat			
Weapon Name	Type	Rarity	Scavenge Cost
Club (nightstick, ASP, bat, crowbar, etc.) *	CQC	-	2
Heavy Club (fire axe, large plank, etc.)	CQC	-	2
Knife *	CQC	-	2
Heavy Blade (machete, sharpened sword, etc.)	CQC	1	3
Miscellaneous Equipment			
Item Name	Type	Rarity	Scavenge Cost
Booze *	Misc	-	2
Medical Supplies *	Misc	-	2

CARDS AND ACCESSORIES

At the back of the book you will find two different kinds of card: Character and, Group and Refuge.

Each Character Card will contain all the information you need for one of the members of your Group. The Group and Refuge card will have all the notes for your current Refuge, any Perks you have, and a space for all your stashed equipment.

Feel free to photocopy as many of these as you need. You can also find them in PDF form online.

SET-UP

SETTING UP THE GAME

Setting up a game of *Last Days* is a pretty uncomplicated four step process. You can play the game on a space not much bigger than the average kitchen table, and this is intentional. *Last Days* is a game that focuses on the life and death struggles of your characters. The smaller the space the encounters takes place in, the more engaged you will be with the game.

Get your models, cards, dice, and tokens together, along with your terrain collection. You may want to make some themed pieces later on, but play at least one game first to get a sense of what you might want to make and how you might want it to look!

THE GAMING TABLE

Last Days is meant to be played on a 3'x3' gaming surface. Whether this is a custom built ruined city or simply a taped off square on your coffee table is irrelevant; whatever works for you! You can easily play it on a smaller or a larger table but I'd suggest adjusting the deployment zones for each Encounter by the differential (for instance, if playing on a 4'x4' space and normal deployment is 3", add 6" to deployment) to get the action going sooner. Likewise, zombies summoned by Noise should arrive deeper onto the table instead of on the deployment edge so they're not left out of the action!

TERRAIN

Where your zombie apocalypse takes place is totally up to you. It could be the abandoned residential sprawl of a minor city, the urban chaos of a large city, or

even the dusty roads of the rural backwoods where people have fled the chaos. Your scenery collection should reflect where you want your campaign to be set, but the more terrain the better. *Last Days* is best played in dense terrain. Ideally, you should fill at least one third of the board with larger pieces of terrain and then spread it out, placing a large piece in the middle to block lines of sight between deployment edges. After that, add scatter terrain such as vehicles, trees, and other furniture to give your Groups more options to hide. Ideally, there should only be a few long lanes of fire with most clear spaces being restricted to about 12".

When you are placing terrain it is important that players agree to what characteristics it might have: for instance, being Open, Difficult, or Climbable. Open terrain should be an easy to move through for a character. Examples such as gentle hills, steps, or roads and paths. Difficult should be harder to traverse such as muddy bogs, rocky inclines, or garbage strewn rooms. Climbable areas should be look as though a character could conceivable scramble up without the use of special equipment. A dumpster next to a concrete building for instance. A sheer wall would not be.

These terms will be important later when it comes to taking actions to move around the board. Use your common sense. If you talk about it now when you're setting up it won't turn into an argument later!

Special scenery features like doors, ladders, and vehicles can have additional rules.

SPECIAL TERRAIN FEATURES

Ladders: Ladders can be used to move up or down quickly. A model using a ladder counts their movement as being through Open Terrain for the purposes of movement (measure vertically). They must have enough AP left to move completely from one place to the next; you cannot 'hang off' ladders. Zombies cannot use ladders.

Doors: Doors can begin the game Open or Closed (decided by the player who places the terrain piece). Models can open or close them by using the appropriate Action. Uncontrolled zombies cannot open doors but can destroy them by attacking them in the CQC Phase, if they are between them and their advance towards their appropriate target model. They are hit automatically and have an Endurance of 4 and 2 Damage Capacity. Once destroyed doors can no longer be closed.

(Optional) Car Alarms: It can be really inconvenient to have these go off when you're standing next to one. They attract every zombie within a mile. If there are any scenery pieces of cars, vans, or trucks (but not transports, school buses, etc) on the table, there is a possibility they have an active car alarm. Roll 1D6 whenever a model within 2 " of a vehicle is shot at (whether they are hit or not). On a 6, the Car Alarm is set off and that piece of scenery counts as having generated 3 Noise Tokens during the next Menace Phase. This can happen multiple times per game!

DEPLOYMENT

As the Groups encounter each other, Leaders will quickly make a plan on how to proceed. Both players should Roll-Off. The winner may decide which table edge they will deploy their Group. Unless stated otherwise by a Scenario, Characters may be deployed anywhere along that edge, up to 3" on to the table. This is called the deployment zone.

After determining which edge their Group will select but before deploying a model, the players should deploy all remaining Supply Tokens on the board (see page 36). The player that did not choose a deployment zone may place a Supply Token first following the rules below. Alternate until they are all deployed.

Once this is done, the player who selected their deployment edge will then deploy their entire Group. The opposing Player will then deploy their own Group using the same deployment rules in the deployment zone opposite.

Once all Supply Tokens are placed, players will deploy their Groups according to the rules outlined above or any additional ways dictated by the Scenario. Everything is set to begin the game.

In a basic game of *Last Days*, set up the board as described above and play until all Supply Tokens have left the table or one side reaches its Breaking Point. If one side Breaks, any Supply Tokens still on the table are considered claimed by the opposing Group unless they themselves Break in the same turn. The Group with the most Supply Tokens is the winner.

SUPPLY TOKENS

Supplies mean survival in the zombie apocalypse. Medicine, canned food, bullets, warm clothes. All of these can mean the difference between life and death. Things that used to be discarded thoughtlessly are now worth killing over.

Supply Tokens are represented by a physical marker. This should be a 1" circular object to keep them easy to deploy. You can use something as simple as a 25mm Base with some bits of appropriate loot modelled on.

Every game of *Last Days* will have at least five Supply Tokens deployed on the table. The first will always be deployed on ground level as close to the center of the board as possible. The other four will be deployed, two per player, anywhere on the table but not within 6" of a table edge, deployment zone, or another Supply Token.

Characters may use the Interact action to pick up or drop a Supply Token if they are in contact with it. Either put it on the Character's card or place it in contact with the Character's model. Supply Tokens have the Heavy 2 rule. Due to their bulky nature, a Character may only carry a single Supply Token at any given time. A Character may also use the Interact action to hand the Supply Token to another Character in their Group with whom they are in Contact.

If a Character is taken Out of Action while carrying a Supply Token, the controlling player may place it in Contact with them before the model is removed.

PLAYING THE GAME

Last Days is a game of, first and foremost, survival. Your Characters have not left their refuge out of curiosity, or a desire to see the world and face its evils. This is not a romantic adventure story. They are leaving the relative safety and security of their chosen safe-zone because if they do not, the group starves. Or is overrun. Or freezes to death. There are a hundred ways to die in this new world surrounded by hungry corpses.

Your Group is competing for resources with everyone else. The game assumes that encounters with friendly survivors or other established groups go relatively unannounced and unrecorded. Narratively, those encounters could represent new Characters joining your Group or even what supplies you return to your Refuge with via barter or trade with friendlier encampments after an encounter.

The Groups you encounter on the tabletop are hostile. For whatever reason, violence erupts and that is where a game of *Last Days* picks up.

In this new 'them-or-us' world you fight… or you die.

THE PHASES

Every game of *Last Days* is divided up into Phases that are completed one after the other and make up the game turn. When the last Phase is complete you return to the first and repeat until the final turn is resolved.

The Phases in a game of *Last Days* are:

1. The Menace Phase
2. The Action Phase
3. The Shooting Phase
4. The Close Quarters Combat Phase
5. The End Phase

This basic five-step-format is the heart of every game you will play, so the familiarizing yourself with this section of the rules before you get into the more complicated stuff, like Campaigns, will make learning to play that much easier.

THE MENACE PHASE

The first (and arguably most important) part of every turn is the Menace Phase. This Phase begins the turn, and is the part of each round where the players really have little to no control. Living in a post-apocalyptic earth infested with the undead is no simple thing. Most survivors learn early on that the best way to stay alive is to stay quiet and unnoticed. Too much noise will attract zombies like moths to a flame! The gunfire and violence of a confrontation between two Groups in a game of *Last Days* is sure to draw the unwanted (or in some cases wanted) attention of the living dead.

This Phase is divided into several sub-steps. The first step is to resolve Noise Tokens. The second step is to resolve Ammo Tokens. The third step is Zombie Activation.

1. Noise Tokens
2. Ammo Tokens
3. Zombie Activation

Each step is resolved as explained below:

NOISE TOKENS

Noise tokens are generated by any model equipped with a Firearm, but can also be a trait that models simply possess. Each time that model takes a shot (so, for each of the Rate of Fire points it uses, as explained in the Shooting section, see page 51) it receives a Noise Token. The player with the most Noise Tokens will resolve this step first for all his models. Roll-Off in the case of a tie.

During this step of the Menace Phase, each model with a Noise Token must roll a die (1D6) and add the number of Noise Tokens they have from the previous turn. Any model that achieves a total of 7 or higher will draw a zombie to the battlefield. Take a zombie model and place it to on the open table edge nearest the model that drew it to the combat zone. It will then be activated just like any other zombie already on the table during the Zombie Activation step. Keep all the cards of models that had Noise Tokens to one side until the end of the Zombie Activation step as zombies can be attracted to sound!

If a model ever has 6 or more Noise Tokens on it during the Menace Phase, it will automatically summon one zombie, and then roll again adding any Noise Tokens it has over 6 to that dice roll. For example, if it had 7 Noise Tokens it would summon one zombie, then Test again adding 1 to the roll.

> Earlier it was recommended you have 20 Zombies on hand for your games of Last Days. This number will rarely be reached during the course of the game, but we recommend you stop rolling for Noise Tokens when it is and only roll for them again once it drops back down below. It will be rare that this large a horde descends on the table, but keeping track of them all can get difficult unless there is an upper limit! You are free to disregard this rule if you want.

AMMO TOKENS

Ammo Tokens represent the consumption of ammunition by a model's weapon during the Shooting Phase. Some weapons with larger magazines can go on firing much longer than others and will have a very high Reload Number. Others will require almost constant reloading. Each time a model uses a Firearm, that Firearm receives an Ammo Token (so, for each of the Rate of Fire points it uses, as explained in the Shooting section). If armed with more than one gun, a model can choose to switch between them each turn. Each gun will accumulate Ammo Tokens individually, and must be rolled for separately to see if they need reloading.

The player with the most Ammo Tokens will resolve this step first for all his models. Roll-Off in the case of a tie.

During this step, each model with an Ammo Token on it must roll a die (1D6) for each of his Firearms and add the number of Ammo Tokens that it has accumulated. If this number is equal or greater to the Firearm's Reload Number then it will require reloading. This is known as an Ammo Roll.

Reloading is an action and is described later in the Action section. Suffice to say, that it can be very inconvenient to be caught out of ammo when surrounded by an advancing horde of the living dead, or pinned down in a firefight!

Unlike Noise Tokens, Ammo Tokens are only removed once a gun is reloaded. That means that they will continue to be accumulated (from one turn to the next) until the turn that the gun clicks to empty, and the model needs to reload it or they reload it voluntarily.

You will always roll for Ammo Tokens, provided you have any, even if you did not accumulate more during a turn. This represents the models panic-firing shots at phantoms and the general disarray of combat.

ZOMBIE ACTIVATION

All Zombies activate during this step of the Menace Phase. The Zombie Activation step represents almost a 'turn within a turn' during which all the zombies on the table are activated one after the other by the players following a strict set of parameters. Zombies activate using exactly the same table as normal models with the exceptions noted later.

Zombies in a game of *Last Days* are simple, mindless things and operate in a predictable way. Roll-Off to see who gets to move a zombie of their choice first.

Knockback Tokens represent non-lethal damage inflicted on the living dead. As described later (see page 61), the undead can only be put down for good by inflicting lethal damage to their brain (Shoot them in the head!). Any other kinds of damage will only slow them down or knock them over, that is represented by Knockback Tokens.

Every time a zombie is hit by a Ranged Attack (not Close Quarters) and survives, it receives a number of Knockback Counters equal to a Firearm's Knockback characteristic. Each Knockback Counter on a zombie subtracts 1 Action Point from their total for the round. As a zombie typically has an Action Points characteristic of 5, it cannot move at all if it has 5 or more Knockback Tokens on it at the beginning of the turn. It is most likely too busy picking itself up off the ground!

Any Knockback Tokens a zombie has in excess of its Action Points characteristic are ignored. It is already on the ground!

Discard all Knockback Tokens a Zombie has at the end of its activation.

Typically, during a game of *Last Days* there will be a small number of Zombies on the table from the start. These represent a few 'roamers', as they're sometimes called, that lurk about waiting for something to feed on. Other zombies can enter the table during combat, attracted by the Noise as described above.

Drawn by the sounds of life (which means tasty brains!) they will be an omnipresent threat for both sides. In games of *Last Days* you don't just worry about your opponent… there are plenty of other things trying to kill you!

THE ACTION PHASE

Once the Menace Phase is over, the Groups begin to maneuver and act as they scramble to both grab supplies, attack and defend themselves from the enemy, and complete any objectives dictated by the Encounter. Activations will pass back and forth between the players so that you will always be maneuvering and reacting to the changing flow of the encounter.

Before activations begin, however, the Initiative must be set for the turn.

THE INITIATIVE ROLL

This simple step will allow the players to determine each turn in what order models will activate and who currently has the upper hand tactically in the remaining Phases.

Each Group in a game of *Last Days* will have a Character in it defined as the Leader. This model is the de-facto commander of this band of survivors and will be the one shouting encouragement and trying to lead the rest of the group to safety or victory.

During the Initiative Step, the Leader of each group will roll a die and add their combined Courage and Intelligence characteristics to the total. The winner may choose to be either the Aggressor or Defender for that turn. In the case of a tie, roll again until there is a clear winner.

The Aggressor has decided that momentum and physical combat are the key to victory this turn and will get to activate a model first in the Action Phase and select a model to attack in the Close Quarter Combat Phase.

The Defender has decided that caution and firepower are to their advantage in this turn and will get to select a model to fire their weapon first during the Shooting Phase.

As being the Aggressor or the Defender both have their advantages, players will need to decide if they want to move and fight first or if they want to shoot first. How wise a plan that is will, ultimately, be up to fate (and the dice!).

LOSS OF THE LEADER

Should the Leader be taken Out of Action (all Damage Capacity removed) during the course of a game, the controlling player must **immediately** nominate the temporary leader of the Group.

This model will gain the Leader skill until the end of the game and must be the model with the next highest combined Courage and Intelligence in the group. In the case of multiple models having the same combined total, the controlling player may choose the model that will take over. Should the Group's Leader die there are additional consequences that will be defined later in the Campaign section.

ACTIVATING MODELS

During the Action Phase both players will get a chance to move their models through the battlefield to gain the advantage of position, get to objectives, or simply run for their lives!

During the previous step one player will have been declared the Aggressor. This Leader has currently taken the initiative and will get to move one of his models before the Defender. There is a downside however, the Defender will later be able to shoot with one of his unengaged models before the Aggressor gets to return fire. A smart player can turn this to his advantage by setting up corridors of fire that his opponent will have to pass through!

It can be useful to put all your active Character cards in a pile and one activated place them face down in a second pile. This will allow you to keep track of what models have activated so far this turn and which ones have not.

THE AGGRESSOR ACTIVATES

As he has won the initiative, the Aggressor picks one of his models and begins spending its Action Points until he decides to stop, or his Action Point total reaches zero for that fighter. All actions must be completed before he begins to move another model. He cannot spend some Action Points on his leader, pass to the Defender and then go back! How Action Points are spent will be explained below. Once he is finished with the first fighter, the Action Phase passes over to the Defender. The two will then alternate activating models and spending Action Points until all models are activated. Action Points may be spent in any order and actions can be taken multiple times per turn.

THE DEFENDER ACTIVATES

The Defender then activates a model in his Group, using the same criteria and restrictions as the Aggressor, detailed above. Both players take turns activating models to completion, passing back and forth.

If a player runs out of models to activate before their opponent, then the player will simply wait while the other side continues activating his remaining models.

SPENDING ACTION POINTS

As explained in the section on Characteristics, Action Points are what models use to perform tasks and get around the battlefield. The possible actions that a model can take with Action Points are detailed in the chart below. Whether or not a model can enter into Contact with an action will be noted in the action's effect.

Models may 'move through' other friendly (but not enemy!) models provided they have enough Action Points to completely clear the other model's base so that they do not overlap.

It is important to note that not all models can perform all actions. Zombies and Characters with the Animal special rule can only perform actions marked with an asterisk (*). Any model in Contact with an enemy model **must** perform a Break Contact action before they can perform any other actions that Phase.

Once both players have completed activating all their Characters in the Action Phase it is time to take aim and fire in the Shooting Phase.

MOVEMENT ACTION TABLE		
Movement Actions	**AP Cost**	**Effect**
Move through Normal Terrain (*)	1 Action Point	The model may move 1" in any direction. It may enter into Contact with this action. It must end in a position where its base will fit and may not move through any gaps that won't accommodate its base.
Move through Difficult Terrain (*)	2 Action Points	The model may move 1" in any direction. It may enter into Contact with this action. It must end in a position where its base will fit and may not move through any gaps that won't accommodate its base.
Run	1 or more Action Points	Model may move AP expended x 2 in inches in any direction, but *only* in a straight line. It may not enter Difficult Terrain, cannot shoot this turn, and generates 1 Noise Token. It must end in a position where its base will fit and may not move through any gaps that won't accommodate its base. It may enter into Contact with this action. Unlike other actions, this action may only be taken once per turn. Place a marker next to the Character to note that they have Run this turn.
Break Contact with the Enemy	3 Action Points, +1 for each enemy in contact after the first.	The model must move 1" directly away from the model(s) it is in Contact with. If it cannot make this move (because of scenery or intervening models) it may not perform this action.
Jump / Fall (*)	2 Action Points per inch of horizontal movement during a Jump Zombies forced to move towards a model with an intervening Gap will automatically Fall.	The model may use their AP to be placed across a raised gap, provided they have enough AP to jump it. They must begin this action at the edge. Do not measure beforehand when you declare a jump. If you do not have the distance to cross, you will fall instead. Place the model at the bottom of the gap. Make a Damage roll with a Strength equal to the number of inches (rounded up) the model falls. It may enter into Contact with this action (including through falling!)
Climb a Climbable Surface (*)	2 Action Points per inch of height.	The model may move from one climbable level to the next. It may enter into Contact with this action.

MOVING OFF THE TABLE

Unless stated otherwise by the Encounter, Characters may leave the board during their movement by moving off any edge. The most common reason for doing this is to escape with Supply Tokens.

MISCELLANEOUS ACTIONS		
Misc. Actions	AP Cost	Effect
Open/Close a Door	2 Action Point	The Door becomes open/closed and can now be/not be moved through.
Reload a Firearm	2 Action Points	The Firearm is reloaded and can now be used as normal. Discard all Ammo Tokens it had on it. This can be done voluntarily, even if the weapon has not yet failed an Ammo Roll.
Go Locked and Loaded	4 Action Points	The model gains a Locked and Loaded Token. Once it has taken this action it may no longer spend Action Points during this Phase. See a full description of Locked and Loaded on page 49.
Interact	3 Action Points	Interact actions are used for Objectives and to do things such as picking up, putting down or passing Supplies. This may not be done if a hostile model is in Contact.

LOCKED AND LOADED

A model which performs the Locked and Loaded action may not perform any further actions during that Action Phase apart from spending their Locked and Loaded Token.

A model with a Locked and Loaded Token may choose to spend it later during the current Action phase, or the subsequent Zombie Activation step of the Menace Phase during the next turn. A Locked and Loaded Token can be spent after a model in Line of Sight and within 12" spends Action Points on a single action. The effect is resolved (for instance, move 1" in open terrain) and then this Character interrupts the opposing player or zombie's spending of AP. They cannot continue to spend them until the Locked and Loaded Token is resolved. Spending it allows that model to make a number of Ranged Attacks up the Rate of Fire of one it its Firearms (that hasn't run out of ammo!). All shots must target the model which triggered the Locked and Loaded Token.

If the target performed a Run action the model firing may decide anywhere along its Run move to target the figure.

Going Locked and Loaded can allow the Character to fire its weapon twice during a turn up to the full Rate of Fire of the weapon. It may also opt to fire different Firearms if it fires later in the turn. It will fire once when it spends its Locked and Loaded Token and once again as normal during the Shooting Phase. Once expended, the token is removed.

If a Character has a Locked and Loaded Token when it is activated it is immediately discarded as the Character's surveillance of the Area ends for that round. It may spend Action Points to gain another one freely during this new activation.

THE SHOOTING PHASE

During this Phase of the game turn, the Characters will get to use their Firearms to try to kill both marauding zombies and each other! Whether or not your Group relies heavily on noisy weapons to defend themselves against their enemies is up to you, but it's hard to deny their effectiveness when attacking the living.

Much like in the Action Phase, it can be useful to put all your unengaged Character cards in a pile and one they have fired their weapon, put them face down in a separate pile to keep track of who has fired and who has not.

MAKING A RANGED ATTACK

In order to make a Ranged Attack a model must have Line of Sight (LOS) to its intended target. Only models and certain pieces of terrain dictated by the scenario are valid to be picked as the intended target. It obviously follows that if a shooter cannot draw LOS to a model, it cannot be declared the target of a Ranged Attack. Finally, the shooter must not be in Contact with any enemy models. Models in Contact may not fire their weapons as they are too busy attacking or defending themselves. Likewise, a model in Contact with a friendly fighter cannot be targeted by a Ranged Attack as survivors are not willing to endanger their companions.

Below is an example entry for a Firearm.

Weapon Name	Class	Range	Damage	ROF	Knockback	Reload	Special Rules
Hunting Rifle	Rifle	24"	3	1	1	6	None

Once a model has been determined to be in Line of Sight you must check whether or not your Firearm is in range. All Firearms have different ranges, as most conventional weapons become inaccurate or lose power over long distances.

If a model is in Line of Sight and range, then you must now determine the dice roll needed to hit your intended target.

Certain criteria can modify a model's Firearms skill before you take your shots, these are:

FIREARMS SKILL MODIFIER TABLE	
Criteria	**FA Modifier**
The target is a Zombie (They don't even try to get out of the way).	+1
The target performed a Run action during its activation.	-1
The target is in cover (obscured Line of Sight).	-1
The Character is firing any Rate of Fire shots after the first (if a Firearm has a ROF of more than 1, the 2nd, 3rd, etc. shots incur this penalty). This penalty is not cumulative on shots after the second (further shots are only ever at -1).	-1

LUCKY 75 – FIREARMS TESTS

Once the final modified Firearms skill of the shooter has been determined, roll 1D6 and add your Firearms skill. This is a Firearms/7 Test.

If the total of the die roll and your Firearms skill is 7 or higher, you have scored a hit!

If modifiers take a model's Firearms skill to 0, then the shot is impossible and automatically misses!

THE DEFENDER FIRES

The Shooting Phase begins with the Defender for this turn choosing one of his models to make Ranged Attacks with. Each Character in a Group may make a number of Ranged Attacks up to the Rate of Fire (RoF) statistic of one chosen Firearm. These attacks can target any enemy model, zombie, or element of scenery allowed by the scenario that they have Line of Sight to. These do not have to be the same models for all the shots and a shooter can go back to a model it has already fired at so long as it still has shots left to fire. Damage is resolved as soon as a hit is made and before the next shot is fired.

Once the model has completed all of its shots (up to the RoF of its gun), the Defender passes shooting over to the Aggressor.

THE AGGRESSOR FIRES

The Aggressor will then fire with one of his Characters using the same procedure and restrictions as the Defender. As mentioned above they will pass back and forth doing so until all models have fired. If a player runs out of members of his Group before his opponent, he will simply wait until his opponent completes shooting with the remaining Characters, activating them one after the other.

RESOLVING SHOOTING DAMAGE

When a Character is hit by a Ranged Attack it may simply take a flesh wound, or it may be killed outright. To see if they receives damage, roll a die (1D6) and add the Damage of the Firearm. This will give you the Damage Total for the attack.

Now divide the Damage Total by the Endurance of the target, rounding down. This is the number of Damage Points inflicted on the target. Mark any Damage on that Character's card.

For Example: *Zeke the Truck Driver hits Steve the Biker with a shot from his Rifle. Zeke rolls to damage and gets a 3. He then adds the Damage of his Rifle (3) to the roll for a Damage Total of 6.*

Steve's endurance is 4… which divides into 6 once rounding down. That means Steve receives one Damage Point.

If Steve's endurance had been 3, it would have divided into the Damage Total twice… resulting in 2 Damage Points.

Once a model's Damage Capacity reaches 0 it is removed from the tabletop as a casualty. The victim may have simply passed out from the pain or they may actually be dead. Regardless they are considered to be Out of Action.

Zombies and damage are handled differently in games of *Last Days*, this will be described later on in their own section (see page 59).

AMMO TOKENS AND RELOADING

As a weapon uses up ammunition it can come to pass that you may exceed the Reload Number in Ammo Tokens (usually during a turn the model has gone Locked and Loaded). Remember that a model does not run out of ammunition until if fails its Ammo Roll during the Menace Phase and may continue to fire until it has done so; even if it has more Ammo Tokens than its Reload Number.

THE CLOSE QUARTERS COMBAT PHASE

During the Close Quarters Combat phase, models can strike blows against each other with whatever's handy: their fists, knives, bats, or in the case of zombies… even their teeth.

The only models who can fight in the Close Quarters Combat Phase are ones in base to base Contact with either an enemy model or zombie as described at the beginning of the rules and in the Action section. If a model is in Contact it must fight and cannot choose not to attack.

The Aggressor picks one of his own models to attack first. The Defender can then pick one of his models using the same criteria. They will then alternate back and forth until all attacks are resolved.

Zombies will attack after all combatants from both sides have finished making their attacks. Which Zombie attacks first is determined in the same way as the player's own models. The Aggressor can choose which will attack first, then the Defender, and back and forth as above.

If a model is removed from the game before it gets to fight (i.e. another fighter is chosen to attack, hits it in combat and then causes enough damage to take it Out of Action) it obviously does not get to fight later on in that Phase.

ATTACKING IN CLOSE QUARTERS COMBAT

Close Quarters Combat is not just a single strike against your enemy; it is a swirling, frantic fight to stay alive. This is an Opposed Test. When a model is chosen to attack it will roll a die (1D6) and add their Close Quarters Combat characteristic, adjusted by any of the modifiers in the table below. The defending model (the one being attacked) will then roll a die (1D6) and do the same.

CQC MODIFIER TABLE	
Criteria	CQC Modifier
Attacking a Zombie	+1
Attacker or Defender is in contact with more than one hostile model	-1 for each model in contact after the first.
Weapon Close Quarters Combat Modifier	See Weapon Profile

The model with the highest total Combat Score is the winner of the fight. If this is the attacker, they may roll to Damage as described below. If this is the defender, they have managed to fend off their assailant but will strike no blows themselves as they are simply focusing on not being hit. Ties will go to the model with the highest CQC characteristic, then if still tied to the Aggressor.

If a model is in contact with more than one hostile model (from the opposing force or a zombie) it must choose which model it is going to attack. The other model(s) do not have to defend, but their presence does cause a penalty as described above.

A Character can never have a CQC of less than 0. Once it reaches 0 simply stop applying penalties.

RESOLVE CLOSE QUARTERS COMBAT DAMAGE

If an attacker wins a combat it may attempt to damage the enemy.

Example Weapon Profile:

Weapon Name	CQC Modifier	Strength Modifier	Special Rules
Club	+/-0	+1	None

When a model is hit by a close combat attack it may simply take a flesh wound, or it may be killed outright. To see if a model receives damage, roll a die and add the Strength of the attacker, plus any modifiers its weapon may add or subtract. This will give you the Damage Total for the attack.

Now divide the Damage Total by the Endurance of the target, rounding down. This is the number of Damage Points inflicted on the target.

For example: *Having dealt with Steve the Biker, Zeke the Truck Driver is at it again, brawling this time with Carl, the former lawyer. Zeke attacks Carl with a tire-iron (Club) and wins the fight. Zeke rolls to damage and gets a 2. He then adds the damage bonus of his club (1) and his strength (3) to the roll for a Damage Total of 6. Carl's endurance is 4... which divide into 6 once rounding down. Carl takes 1 Damage Point.*

If Carl's endurance had been 3 it would have divided into the Damage Total twice... resulting in 2 Damage Points.

Once a model's Damage Capacity reaches 0 it is removed from the tabletop as a casualty, just like with shooting. The victim may have simply been stunned, knocked out cold, or they may actually be dead. This is called going 'Out of Action'. Zombies and damage are handled differently in games of *Last Days*, which will be described later on in their own section (see page 59).

THE END PHASE

The End Phase divides one game turn from another. It is used to check whether or not one group has defeated the other based on the victory conditions outlined by the Encounter. Certain effects generated by traits are often resolved in the End Phase as well.

BREAKING POINT

Checking to see if your Group of survivors has reached the Breaking Point is something a Leader may be required to do every turn. It is not a Phase, but rather something that divides the end of one turn from the beginning of the other.

During any turn that a Group took at least one casualty, it must Test to see if the fighters have reached their Breaking Point at the end of the Close Quarters Phase. Starting with the Aggressor for that turn, roll a die (1D6) and add the number of casualties the group has taken. If that number is less than or equal to the combined Courage characteristic of the Group's Leader and the remaining number of friendly fighters still on the table, then they will continue to fight. If that number is greater than that total, then they will flee and the game will end.

If a Leader does not have a Courage characteristic (if for example, he has a Horror characteristic instead), he must use his Intelligence characteristic for this roll.

A Leader may choose to automatically fail this roll at the end of any turn after the second, so long as they have taken at least one casualty that round.

If one Group reaches their Breaking Point and the other does not, then the Group still on the table is the winner of the scenario regardless of the objective. If both Groups hit their Breaking Point in the same turn, then the scenario is a draw.

Obviously if all the models in a Group are Out of Action when this roll is required, then they will automatically fail. However, the other side is still required to Test if they suffered casualties in that turn, as the game could still be a draw.

ZOMBIES

Zombies are a fact of life in the hopeless future of *Last Days*. These mindless rotting cannibals will always be present in your games so it's important you know their capabilities. You can manipulate these dangerous ghouls to your advantage, if you know exactly what they do.

The following special rules apply to all basic zombies, the kind that will be attracted to the table by noise, and begin on the table in some scenarios.

THE ZOMBIES OF THE LAST DAYS

Zombies in games of *Last Days* are slow zombies. They are the classic zombies of the films of the sixties and seventies, not the more modern fast zombies of more recent films. These may have existed during the early days of infection, but the infected have slowed as their bodies have begun to rot. This distinction is important to make because it defines how they work in the game. One-on-one, a zombie and a human survivor are not evenly matched… but they are dangerous in groups!

ZOMBIE CHARACTERISTICS

Zombies in *Last Days: Zombie Apocalypse* have the following characteristics:

ZOMBIE

AP	CQC	FA	S	E	DC	H	I
5	2	0	3	*	1	3	0

Equipment	None, apart from a horrible stench and the rags in which they died
Special Rules	You've got to shoot them in the head!

MOVING ZOMBIES

Zombies move only in the Menace Phase of the game turn as described earlier.

Zombies will always move towards the nearest non-zombie model to which they have Line of Sight. It will spend **all** available Movement Points attempting to get into Contact with that model so that it may fight during the Close Quarters Phase. If it is already in Contact with a non-zombie model it will do nothing but wait to attack later on. If there are no living models in Line of Sight, then the zombie will move towards the closest model that Tested for a Noise Token during that Menace Phase (regardless of Line of Sight), attempting to break through doors if doing so would get them there more quickly. If no such model exists the zombie idles and does not move.

If the closest non-zombie model cannot be reached, because another zombie (or zombies) is already engaging it and in the way, the zombie must move towards the next closest model that is unengaged (and to which it has Line of Sight) instead. If no such model exists, it behaves exactly as if it had no Line of Sight at all.

Remember to adjust the Action Points total of the zombie upon activation by the number of Knockback Tokens they received the following turn, and then to discard them at the end of its activation.

Also note that all zombies can only perform those actions marked with an asterisk (*) in the Action Phase, as described earlier (see page 47).

ZOMBIES IN COMBAT

Zombies are slow, ponderous things. They are completely without the ability to reason and as such cannot operate or use Firearms. Any zombies in contact with the enemy will attack as described earlier, after all living combatants have fought. Of course if they're killed before they get to do so they may not fight.

The Aggressor may choose in which order to resolve Close Quarters Combat with uncontrolled zombies.

You will notice that zombies do not have the Endurance characteristic. The reason for this is simple, they're dead! Zombies have the special rule 'Shoot them in the head!'.

SPECIAL RULE: SHOOT THEM IN THE HEAD!

Instead of making a Damage roll against a model with this attribute when they are hit by Shooting or Close Quarters Combat, roll a die (1D6). On a roll of 5 or 6 the model has been hit in the head and the brain has been destroyed. It takes 1 Damage Point. As this rule typically applies to zombies, this will usually mean that they are removed from the game. Do not forget that if the damage roll was caused by a Ranged Attack, then on a roll of 1 to 4 the model with this special rule will accumulate a number of Knockback tokens equal to the Knockback statistic of the weapon being fired.

HORROR AND COURAGE

The zombie apocalypse is a very scary place to live. You can't go to sleep without first assuring your safety and that you are not going to awaken to a corpse chewing on your leg.

Horror and Courage are opposed characteristics. Some models (usually living ones) will have a Courage characteristic. This represents their ability to cope with the terrifying situations in which they may find themselves.

Other models (mostly the living dead) will have a Horror characteristic. This represents how frightening they are to others.

These characteristics come into play when a model with a Horror characteristic makes it into Contact with a model with the Courage characteristic. Both models must roll a die (1D6) and add their respective characteristic. If the model entering into Contact is a zombie, have the opposing player make the roll for it.

If the Horror causing model's total is greater than that of the model it is engaging, it will panic as it grapples with the undead and may not use Action Points to break off for the remainder of the turn. The model is assumed to be simply fighting for its life instead. This makes zombies 'Sticky', a real threat when they appear in large numbers as they can slowly overwhelm the living in their panic.

Obviously Horror causing models have no effect on models that also cause Horror, and likewise Courageous models have no effect on other Courageous models.

SPECIAL RULES

Characters in games of *Last Days* can have a variety of things that make them unique. These can be skills and abilities that they may begin with or learn during a Campaign. They can also be the innate attributes that make up what or who a model is. These things come in two categories: skills and attributes. Skills are typically something you learn or train to do in games of *Last Days*. Models may begin with them as specialists in a Group or they may learn them as part of a Campaign. Attributes are physical traits either inherent to a model or passed on by a piece of equipment or event during the game. It is important to note that pieces of equipment may have attributes that effect your models, so make note if they do!

SKILLS

AGRICULTURALIST

This Character's green-thumb means any growing and preserving of food done by the Group yields a far greater surplus than if it were tended by an untrained hand. If this Character is sent to work the Fenced-In Garden Perk of a Refuge, they may roll 2D6 to see how many Scavenge Points they generate instead of just one.

AMBUSHERS

Surprise can mean the difference between victory and defeat in a world without laws or consequences. This Character knows how to spot avenues of advance that will put Group members in the right place to catch their enemies unaware. During deployment, nominate between 1 and 3 Characters in your Group. Make an Intelligence/6 Test. If it is passed, when deploying the first model selected they may be placed anywhere within 6" of the neutral sides of the board, not within your opponent's half. If the Test is failed, they get lost. They may not participate in this game but are unharmed and arrive safely back at the Refuge later on. Increase the difficulty of this roll by 1 for the second and 2 for the third models selected. (Intelligence/7 and Intelligence/8 Tests respectively).

CROWD CONTROL

This Character is an expert at using his opponent's numbers against them. He ignores the negative CQC penalty for being in contact with multiple hostile models.

DIRTY FIGHTER

Even in an absolute struggle for life or death it is hard for most people to truly, savagely attack another living being. This Character has no such compunctions and will use any advantage they can. In the case of a tie in an opposed CQC Test involving this model, they will be considered the winner and cause a Damage roll, even if they were defending. If both models have this skill, then the result is still a tie.

DISARM

This Character knows that an enemy without their weapon is far less dangerous than an enemy with a weapon. If this fighter wins an Opposed CQC Test against an opponent armed with any type of weapon it may roll a Strength/6 Test instead of making a Damage roll. If successful, the model hit has a single weapon removed from its card for the rest of this game.

DOUBLE-TAP

One in the chest and one in the head is the mantra of this Character. They may expend 1 extra Ammo and Noise Token to re-roll a Damage or Shoot them in the Head! roll with a Firearm each time they inflict a hit in the Shooting Phase. They must accept the second result, even if it is worse than the first.

FIRST AID TRAINING

This Characters knows a bit about basic emergency medicine and will do their best with whatever is around to keep their teammates alive. If this fighter is not Out of Action at the end of the game, they will allow you to re-roll one of the two dice rolled on the Injury chart in the Campaigns section. The second die roll must stand and cannot be re-rolled again. If you have two Characters with this skill however, their combined efforts **can** be used to re-roll the other die. This must be decided upon before either die is re-rolled. A Character can only use this skill once between each game.

ENGINEER

When it comes to planning, expanding, or reinforcing the Group's Refuge, this Character has skills that can make backbreaking work simpler, easier, and more efficient, with the results being better and more durable. When assigned to build a new Perk in a Refuge, this model reduces the cost of the Perk by 25% (round up the nearest Scavenge Point).

ENTRY MAN

Obstacles, like doors, provide little defense against this Character. A model with this skill may spend a single AP while in contact with a basic, non-reinforced door. Make a Strength/6 Test. If passed, this door is destroyed and removed from the game.

FIRE AND MANEUVER

This Character has become adept at moving while putting the enemy under fire. Every time they make a Ranged Attack against an enemy model they may immediately move 1", provided they do not move through a barrier or through difficult terrain. The movement may be in any direction and may be done up to the Rate of Fire of the weapon being fired, up to a maximum of 3" in one Shooting Phase. The weapon must be fired at an enemy target in order to gain the movement, and can't just be blasted into the air.

FREE RUNNER

Highly athletic, this survivor can perform some incredible physical feats: running up walls, jumping from rooftops, and generally making a mockery of obstacles in his way. Models with this skill pay only 1 AP to move through difficult terrain or to climb a climbable surface (per inch of height). In addition, the model may spend 3 APs to perform a Long Jump. This must be in a straight line, must not pass through models or obstacles, and must not end in difficult terrain. The model may move up to 6", ignoring gaps or difficult terrain (e.g. from a rooftop to another rooftop). The model may travel down up to 3" with this movement but may not travel up. Once it has performed a long jump, it may no longer spend APs for the rest of the turn on any action that causes it to move. Long Jumps cannot be performed if the model attempting it suffers any penalties from the Heavy special rule.

FRONTLINE FIGHTER

When this Character wades into a melee he inspires everyone around him to fight a little bit harder and keep going, even when all seems lost. If this models is within 6" of a friendly Character that is engaged in CQC, they may add +1 to their CQC Characteristic. The model with this skill does not gain the benefit themselves.

GEAR-HEAD

There isn't a lot about cars, trucks, and automobiles that this Character doesn't know. Whenever an Encounter calls for a model to take Interact actions on any type of vehicle, this Character may roll two dice when taking Intelligence Tests and choose whichever of the two results they wish.

GUNFIGHTER

This Character has learned to wield two Firearms (one in each hand). This may only be done with Pistols or SMGs. This allows the fighter to make Ranged Attacks with both Firearms in the same Shooting Phase, up to the Rate of Fire of each gun. The downside is that even the initial shots with each gun incur the -1 FA penalty for firing additional shots.

GUNSMITH (FIREARM CLASS)

The Character is well trained in the operations and science of Firearms. They tinker with their weapons constantly, and also scavenges or makes their own hi-powered ammunition. This rule must only apply to a single Firearm Class chosen when the skill is generated (Pistol, Rifle, etc). Firearms of that Class carried by this Character gain +1 to its Damage, but suffers -1 to its Reload Number due to the smaller supply of available ammunition.

HEADHUNTER

An expert in removing, crushing, or stabbing skulls. This character has mastered one of the most important survival skills in the world of *Last Days*; how to efficiently kill a zombie. All CQC Attacks against zombies gain +1 Lobotomizer in addition to any provided by other sources. In addition, if put on Watch after a game, they add +2 to the roll to drive off the zombies during an attack instead of the normal +1.

HEAVY LIFTER

A Character with this skill can ignore up to 1 point of the Heavy attribute. So, if it was carrying 2 items with the Heavy 1 attribute it would only lose 1 Action Point in each Action Phase.

INSPIRATIONAL PRESENCE

This fighter reassures and encourages the rest of his group of survivors. Any friendly model that is required to take a Courage Test (not the model with this skill) gains a temporary bonus of +1 to their Courage characteristic if they are within 6" of the model with this skill. Multiple instances of this skill are cumulative. Models with this skill do not benefit from being within 6" of themselves, but may benefit from others.

LEADER

Whether naturally charismatic or brutally domineering, a model with this skill is in charge of this group of survivors. If a Leader is within 6" of a friendly model with the Courage characteristic, they may use his Courage value instead of their own for Horror Tests (they are not required to if the Leader's is lower).

MARTIAL ARTS

Whatever form or discipline it takes, this Character has been trained in unarmed combat. This not only gives him the benefit of being quite deadly in Close Quarters Combat, but also making him exceptionally difficult to hit as he is adept at defending himself as well. So long as this Character is not equipped with any Close Combat weapons, it receives a +1 modifier to Damage enemies and any hostile models that attack them suffer a -1 to their CQC characteristic.

QUICK-LOAD

A Character with this ability has a natural affinity for Firearms and can reload their weapons in a flash. The reloading action costs one less AP than it normally would.

RALLYING CRY

When all seems lost, this Character can pull his Group together for one final push towards victory. Once per game, you may re-roll a failed Breaking Point Test. You may only re-roll one of these Tests each game regardless of how many Characters in your group possess this skill.

SCAVENGER

This Character knows perhaps a little too much about breaking and entering or where best to find certain items. If they carried a Supply Token off the board, then in the post-game sequence they allow you to modify one of the two rolls on the Scavenge chart by +1/-1.

SITUATIONAL AWARENESS

This Character has an almost sixth-sense about what is around him and an uncanny ability to spot a trap or hostile groups lying in wait. If they are targeted by an enemy Character with a Locked and Loaded Token, then those two Characters make an opposed Intelligence Test. If the character with this skill wins, the Locked and Loaded Token is lost but that model still generates Ammo and Noise Tokens up to its full Rate of Fire as the Character bluffs them into firing at a distraction. If it they lose the Test, the Locked and Loaded Token is resolved as normal.

SNIPER

Headshots are kill-shots and a vital skill in the world filled with zombies. this Character aims at the head and gains +1 Lobobotomizer to any Ranged Attacks it makes, in addition to any provided by other sources. Also, if put on Watch after a game, they add +2 to the roll to drive off the zombies during an attack instead of the normal +1.

SPRINTER

You learn to be fast in a world of lurking cannibals. A model with this skill gains an additional bonus Action Point each Action Phase that can **only** be spent on the Move or Move through Difficult Terrain actions (it needs to be combined with a normal Action Point for the latter). Calculate this into the distance of a Run action.

STALKER

Moving quickly and quietly is this something that comes naturally to this Character. They do not generate Noise Tokens when they run.

SUBDUE

Trained, perhaps, by a lifetime as a police officer or maybe cracking heads at the local club, this Character is an expert at temporarily pinning down or restraining their foes. Instead of attacking in the CQC Phase, if they are only engaged with a single hostile model they may make an opposed Strength Test. If they pass and if that enemy has not yet attacked this CQC Phase, they may not do so. Instead they grapple to free themselves or get back to their feet. They may attack normally next turn, provided they are not subdued again. If the Test is failed, nothing happens.

TACTICAL ACUMEN

This Character has a flair for combat theory and can take advantage of the ebb and flow of an engagement. If this model is the group's Leader, they may roll two dice for the Initiative Roll and choose whichever is more advantageous. If they are not the Leader, this may only be done if they are within 3 inches of the Leader when the Initiative roll is made. This extra die may only be added once, regardless of how many models with this skill are in range.

TAG-TEAM

Never send one man to do the work of two! This Character is exceptionally good at communicating and acting in concert with the other members of their Group. While within 3" of a friendly Character with the same Keyword that has not yet activated this turn, they may spend 1 Action Point to take this action and perform an Intelligence/6 Test. If passed, when this Character's activation is complete, the second Character may immediately activate as normal. This interrupts the normal back and forth of activation during the Action Phase. Once the second Character's activation is complete, play returns to normal. A player may only use this skill once per turn, even if multiple Characters possess it.

ATTRIBUTES

EXPLOSIVE X

A piece of equipment with this attribute causes damage over an area instead of simply hitting a single model. It still must target a model as normal. If it hits, you must then make a Damage roll against all (including friendly!) models within X inches of the model targeted (where X is listed in the weapons entry). Treat the model originally hit as source of these additional Ranged Attacks. If the space between this point and a model is completely blocked by solid scenery, do not make a Damage roll for them.

FIRE

This weapon leaves a large area of fire when it is used. This is useful to block the advance of the undead or make it impossible for enemy Characters to move through an area. Unlike normal attacks, a weapon with this trait may target any point on the ground within Line of Sight and range of the shooter by passing a Firearms/7 Test. If passed, place a 1" Token on that point. Any model in Explosive range is hit as normal. The marker remains in place until the End Phase of the following turn. Any model beginning its activation, or entering the Explosive range (measured from the Token), will take another hit as the fire continues to burn. If the Test is failed, the weapon fails to ignite and nothing happens.

HEAVY X

This weapon or piece of equipment is particularly heavy and hard to lug around. As long as it is equipped by a Character, they must pay a penalty of -X Action Points at the beginning of each Action Phase. This takes effect before determining the distance of a Run Action.

HIGHLY SPECIALIZED

This weapon may only be operated by someone with the Gunsmith skill. The skill does not have to be attached to that particular Firearm Class, they must simply possess the skill to indicate their intimate knowledge of firearms.

LOBOTOMIZER X

This weapon is particularly handy at busting open zombie heads. It may add up to X to the die roll when attempting to damage a model with the Shoot them in the head! attribute.

NOISY X

A character, weapon, or piece of equipment with this attribute generates +X additional Noise Tokens whenever it is used (each time it is selected to fire, not per ROF or every time it is used in CQC). If a model has this attribute itself, it generates these Noise Tokens during the beginning of its activation.

ONE-USE

This weapon can only be used once and is then removed from the Character's roster sheet.

POINT BLANK

This weapon fires a spread of shrapnel, making it very effective at close range. Models firing this weapon at a target within 3" gains a bonus of 2 points to their Firearms skill for that shot.

SILENT

This weapon has either been fitted with a Silencer, or makes very little noise when being fired. It will not generate Noise Tokens during the game.

SLOW LOADING

Due to the size of the magazine or the complexity of the mechanism, this weapon costs 1 additional Action Point to reload (typically making it 3APs). This can be combined with the Quick-load skill for a net reload cost of 2 Action Points.

STEPPED FIRE

This weapon becomes significantly more dangerous the closer it is to the intended target. Its range will have multiple steps, as will its damage and Knockback. Use the appropriate damage and Knockback for the range at which you are firing it.

THROWN

Thrown weapons do not have a range. Instead, a weapon with the Thrown attribute relies on the Strength of the person using it. Maximum range of a thrown weapon is three times the Strength of the model throwing it.

WEAPONS, EQUIPMENT, AND REFUGE PERKS

In this section you will find described all of the weapons, gear and gizmos that can be found, scavenged, or looted in the world of *Last Days*. In one-off games you will only have access to the basic equipment lists available to your force. In Campaign games you will be able to search for and, hopefully, find all kinds of strange weapons and equipment that will enable your crew of survivors to live a little longer.

WEAPONS

FIREARMS

Man has spent centuries inventing ever more ingenious ways of killing one-another. Even the most anti-gun lobbyist was glad for this proliferation when the dead started returning to life and feasting on the living.

Guns and ammunition are some of the most sought-after commodities in this hostile new world and knowing which one to use at the right time will save a survivor's life day-by-day.

FIREARMS TABLE

Weapon Name	Class	Range	Damage	RoF	Knockback	Reload	Special Rules
Revolver*	Pistol	12"	3	1	1	6	
Semi-Automatic*	Pistol	12"	3	2	1	10	
Magnum*	Pistol	12"	4	1	2	6	Noisy 1
Surplus SMG	SMG	12"	3	3	1	6	
Military SMG*	SMG	18"	3	3	1	8	
Hunting Rifle	Rifle	24"	3	1	1	6	
High-powered Rifle*	Rifle	30"	4	1	2	4	Noisy 1,
Military Sniper Rifle*	Rifle	30"	4	1	2	6	Noisy 1, Lobotomizer 1, Highly Specialized
Surplus Assault Rifle	Rifle	18"	4	2	2	10	Noisy 1
Military Assault Rifle*	Rifle	24"	4	3	2	12	
Sawn off/Breech Loading Shotgun	Shotgun	3/6/9"	6/4/2	1	3/2/1	2	Stepped Fire, Point Blank
Pump-Action Shotgun*	Shotgun	6/12/18"	6/4/3	1	3/2/2	5	Stepped Fire, Point Blank
Combat Shotgun*	Shotgun	6/12/18"	6/4/4	2	3/2/3	5	Stepped Fire, Point Blank
Squad Automatic Weapon*	Heavy	24"	5	4	2	15	Noisy 1, Heavy 1, Slow Reload, Highly Specialized
Minigun*	Heavy	18"	5	6	1	20	Noisy 2, Heavy 2, Slow Reload, Highly Specialized,
Hunting Bow	Sporting	9/18"	3/2	1	0	2	Lobotomizer 2, Stepped Fire, Silent
Hunting Crossbow	Sporting	12/24"	4/3	1	0	2	Lobotomizer 2, Stepped Fire, Silent
Thrown Explosive*	Explosive	*	4	1	5	*	Explosive 3, One-Use, Thrown, Noisy 2
Fire Bomb	Explosive	*	3	1	1	*	Explosive 3, One-Use, Thrown, Noisy 1, Fire

CQC WEAPONS

In the early days of infection most survivors had to make-do with whatever was handy to defend themselves against the newly undead. The majority of them have come to trust in what later became a popular proverb amongst groups of survivors, 'Machetes don't need reloading.'

CLOSE QUARTERS WEAPONS TABLE			
Weapon	CQC Modifier	Strength Modifier	Special Rules
Chainsaw	-1	4	Noisy 2, Heavy 2, Lobotomizer 2
Club *	0	1	None,
Heavy Blade	1	2	Lobotomizer 1
Heavy Club	-1	3	Heavy 1, Lobotomizer 1
Knife*	1	+/-0	Lobotomizer 1,

GENERAL EQUIPMENT

General equipment are non-weapon items that you can buy or scavenge for your group to make use of during games. Most are not available during the creation of your Group due to their scarcity. You will have to find them when you inventory the Supply Tokens that you acquire during games.

ASSAULT ARMOUR [HEAVY 1] [*]

This full bodysuit of heavy Kevlar is issued to riot-police, special forces, and SWAT/ETF. As it covers the arms and legs it provides a bonus of +2 Endurance against damage from both Ranged and Close Quarters Attacks, but confers a penalty of -1 Action Points at the beginning of each Action Phase as it has the Heavy 1 attribute. May not be combined with other armour.

BOOZE [*]

Nothing puts the horror of a world of living corpses to rest like a stiff drink. Any Character equipped with this may choose to use it at the beginning of the game. The model will receive a +1 bonus to their CQC, Endurance, and Courage characteristics for the entire game, but will suffer a penalty of -1 to their Action Points, Firearms, and Intelligence characteristics as well. This item is one-use.

CLIMBING GEAR [*]

This rope and grapple can be used once per game to create an ad-hoc one-level ladder. Place a marker at the bottom of the terrain piece you will be climbing. It will remain there for the rest of the game and can be used by any non-zombie models (friendly or enemy). This item is one-use.

MEDICAL SUPPLIES [*]

Disinfectant, bandages, and painkillers can mean the difference between infection and death in this world without 911 and hospitals. As long as the model equipped with Medical Supplies is not Out of Action at the end of the game, they may use this equipment to adjust the total roll on the Injuries table up or down by one (e.g. an 8 to a 7 or a 10 to an 11). It can be used for secondary rolls. Yes, this can avoid a 'Dead' result! This can be combined with the First Aid Training skill to alter the final result **after** dice have been re-rolled. This item is one-use.

MOD-KIT

Popular at gun-shows as a way to get around the legality of purchasing certain Firearms. These kits will convert one weapon type to another. If used on a Hunting Rifle, it will convert it to a Surplus Assault Rifle. If used on a Semi-Automatic, it will convert it to a Surplus SMG. Both weapons suffer a -1 to their Reload characteristic as they are non-standard conversions. This item is one-use.

NOISEMAKERS

This could be an old alarm clock, some lady-finger fireworks, or any number of other home-made inventions. A Character equipped with this item may place a 1" Token in Contact with itself for 1 AP. During the next Menace Phase this Token produces Noise/5. This item is one-use.

REFLEX SIGHT [*]

This piece of equipment can be mounted to the following Firearm classes: SMGs and Rifles. So long as it is equipped the Character firing the weapon may ignore the -1 penalty for additional ROF shots unless it is using the Gunfighter skill.

RIOT SHIELD [HEAVY 1] [*]

Most commonly seen issued to SWAT/ETF entry teams and counter-terrorist military forces, this heavy shield can be used to block incoming fire and to defend at close quarters. This shield confers cover versus Ranged Attacks regardless of whether the model is in the open or not. It confers no bonus if the model is actually in cover. If the model is defending against a Close Quarters Attack it gains a bonus of +2 to its Close Quarters Combat capability. It gains no bonus when attacking. This shield is cumbersome however, and confers a penalty of -1 Action Points at the beginning of each Action Phase to the bearer as it has the Heavy 1 attribute.

SCOPE [*]

This piece of equipment can be equipped to the following Firearm classes: SMGs and Rifles. So long as it is equipped it grants that weapon the Lobotomize 1 ability as it helps pick out headshots.

SILENCER [*]

Silencers may be equipped to the following classes of Firearm: Pistol, SMG, and Rifle. They provide that weapon with the Silent special rule for that game only. This item is one-use.

TACTICAL VEST [*]

Often issued to police and security guards, this vest does not impede the movement of the wearer, and offers a bonus of +2 Endurance against damage from Ranged Attacks. It provides no benefit against damage from Close Quarter Combat Attacks. May not be combined with other armour.

REFUGE PERKS

Every Refuge has advantages built-in which attract groups to take shelter there in the first place. Some can be added later on as the Characters settle in and make what improvements to the structure.

ARMOURY

To the layman, it might look like having tons of boxes of bullets and weapons everywhere would be a good thing. In reality, unorganized ammunition is a liability in a firefight as people are grabbing the wrong sized rounds for their weapons. A well inventoried and organized armoury means everyone has the right magazines at the right time. If a Character works the Armoury, during the next Encounter their Group may re-roll 3 failed Ammo Rolls. The second result must be accepted.

BUNK BEDS

Sleeping accommodations might not sound like a big deal, that is, until someone gets left outside with the zombies. Building bunk beds means the Refuge can accommodate one extra Character. For each Bunk Bed Perk increase the Maximum Group Size of the Refuge by 1.

ESCAPE VEHICLE

Even the best fortified refuge can suffer the predations of massive hordes of the undead or the assault of hostile groups. Having a Plan-B means if the worst should occur the group doesn't have to leave behind their resources. Whatever new Refuge they end up in, they may keep all of their equipment and weapons in the Group's stash.

FENCED-OFF GARDEN

The cans of scavenged beans and cream of mushroom soup won't last forever. A smart Group will begin to grow and harvest their own food to supplement what they can find by scavenging. If a Character works this Perk the Group may collect D6 Scavenge Points between each game. This Perk may be built multiple times.

FENCES

A good sturdy fence will keep zombies at arm's length for easy disposal and provide at least a deterrent to hostile groups. Zombies do tend to build up at the fences however, which can provide a handy deterrent to enemy Groups. During the Home Defense Encounter you can deploy up to 24" of fences (2" tall, climbable) at least 6" away from Refuge and not more than 8" away. These do not have to be a single line of fence. Additionally, the standard zombies plus D3 additional ones are deployed outside the fences to represent the build-up of undead.

FORTIFIED WINDOWS

While barred windows don't particularly help to stop bullets, they will confound the undead trying to assault the Refuge. Windows are natural weak points during a zombie attack and having them reinforced provides a distinct advantage. During a Zombie Attack the Group may add +1 to the Attack Roll.

INFIRMARY

Having a dedicated space for triage and to provide medical care to wounded Group members both speeds up their recovery and keeps them in a central location to defend during attacks. Each Infirmary in your Refuge can accommodate one Out of Action Character. That Character does not impose the normal -1 to the Zombie Attack Roll. This Perk may be built multiple times.

RADIO ROOM

Being able to coordinate with the Group while they are outside of the Refuge means the scattered Characters can come together in a more organized manner during Encounters. If a Character is assigned to work this Perk they may make an Intelligence/8 Test. If passed, you may modify the Scenario roll by +1 or -1 after it is made. If both Groups have a Radio Room and pass this Test, the Scenario roll may not be modified.

REINFORCED DOORS

Adding a stronger frame, metal plating, and drop-bars to the exterior doors will work equally well to deter zombies and hostile humans. During the Home Defense Encounter, the doors of the Refuge have +1 Damage Capacity and cannot be removed by the Entry Man skill.

SOLID STRUCTURE

Old buildings are often made of stone and mortar as opposed to plastic and wood. Just like in ancient times, these structures are more easily defended and provide better cover against attack. In building terms, this can be accomplished in modern structures with sandbags and bricks to add additional protection from Firearms. During the Home Defense Encounter, Characters taking cover behind the walls of a Refuge with this perk may benefit from better cover, which imposes a -2 to the enemy's Firearm Characteristic, instead of the normal -1.

STORE ROOM

Keeping supplies organized and inventoried means not only does the Group know what they have, they know where it is when they need it. Seemingly valueless items might be worth more in trade later and knowing where they've been stashed can be key. A Group with a Store Room can re-roll one of the die rolls when inventorying Supply Tokens to determine how many Scavenge points it earns. The second result must be accepted.

WATCH TOWER

A good vantage point can give early warning to the Group when the impending zombie attack arrives or an enemy Group is about to launch an assault. If a Character is assigned here during the Zombie Attack they may make an Intelligence/8 Test to re-roll one of the two dice during the Attack Roll. During a Home Defense Encounter deploy a piece of Scenery to represent the Watch Tower (Climbable, at least 6" tall) either on or within 3" of the Refuge. One model may be deployed on the Watch Tower and will always count as being in cover while deployed there.

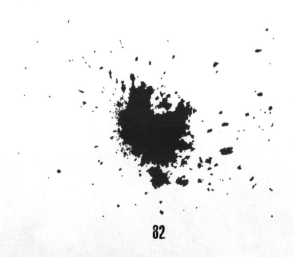

THE CAMPAIGN

Last Days is best enjoyed through playing a Campaign. Campaigns link together individual games and allow the fighters in your group to earn experience and learn new skills. You can scavenge for new equipment and follow their progress through the horrifying terrors of their survival during the zombie apocalypse.

This section will detail the rules for doing this. The narrative that goes along with it is up to you to create and enjoy.

There is more to surviving in the zombie apocalypse than one good run of scavenging against a rival Group. The realities of life where millions of reanimated bodies desire nothing less than to feast on your flesh every hour of every day is a constant, day and night, struggle.

Even after arriving back at their Refuge, your Group will need to work to keep it secure. The zombies will come. They will need to be driven off. It's inevitable.

After each game your Characters will deal with the injuries they suffered during their encounter, earn new skills and abilities by spending experience to Level Up and then be assigned tasks back at the refuge.

INJURIES

The world of *Last Days* is a very, very dangerous place. From the constant attacks of the infected to the rival groups trying to survive there are a lot of ways to die. At the end of each game you must roll on the following chart for any members of your Group that were taken Out of Action (lost all their Damage Points) during the game. You do not need to roll for those Group members still standing, it is assumed they grit their teeth and work through the pain of their flesh-wounds.

2D6 Roll	Injury
	INJURY TABLE
2	**Dead!** This Group member has succumbed to their wounds. Remove them from the Groups roster. All equipment they are carrying is lost to the wasteland.
3	**Captured.** Your Group member has been captured during the game. You may choose to automatically play the Rescue Encounter against that Group as your next game. If you are successful, you get your Group member back with his equipment intact. If you lose or choose not to play the Rescue Encounter, your opponent may keep his equipment and leave him to die (he is automatically killed) at the hands of the undead.
4	**Arm Injury.** Your Group member has lost the use of one of their arms (either amputated, broken and not set properly, etc). He may no longer use any weapons that require more than one hand. This limits them to using only one each of Pistols, SMGs, Thrown, and CQC weapons. Also, they may no longer carry two of each type of weapon. If this result is rolled again, the Character will no longer be able to carry weapons and will count as Dead.
5	**Blinded in One Eye.** The Character has lost an eye, causing them to have problems with depth perception. They suffer a permanent -1 penalty to their Firearms characteristic. If this result is rolled again, the Character is blinded and counts as Dead as they can no longer fight and become a liability.
6–8	**Full Recovery.** The Character has recovered without any long term side-effects.
9	**Shell-Shocked.** Traumatized by their experience, the Character is palsied and unable to act quickly. They suffers a permanent -1 penalty to their Action Point characteristic.
10	**Leg Injury.** Whether badly broken or lost completely, this Character can no longer move around quickly. They must spend an additional Action Point to perform any of the following: Move Through Normal Terrain and Move Through Difficult Terrain. If this result is rolled again they will count as Dead.
11	**Infected!** This Character has fallen victim to the Z-Germ! Roll a single die: on a 1–3 the virus takes hold and their comrades are forced to put them down, treat as a Dead! result. On a 4–6 they are able to amputate the bite area quickly enough. Roll another die: on a 1–3 they suffer an Arm Injury and on a 4–6 they suffer a Leg injury.
12	**I'm Never Doing That Again…** This brush with death has taught the fighter a valuable lesson. He is considered to have rolled a Full Recovery and gains an additional 1D6 Experience Points.

DEATH OF THE LEADER

Should your Leader die your Group may change drastically. During the Refuge and Recuperation stage of the post-game-sequence, you **must** recruit a new Leader and may do so even without having a Leader to assign to that Job. This Leader will not cost any Scavenge Points, but you will need to pay for whatever weapons and equipment he joins the Group with.

This Character is the Group's new savior. They appear at the eleventh hour and pull together the despondent group members mourning the loss of their previous Leader. This Leader **does not** have to have the same Keyword as the previous Leader if you do not wish. This can, however, lead to radical restructuring of the Group as the new Leader will dismiss as many Characters as required to make the Group obey the normal rules for its composition. Those Characters dismissed will take their weapons and equipment with them when they leave. They are considered to be unleadable by someone whose viewpoints are so opposite to their own. This new Leader is treated just like any other Character hired during this later stage and may not have a Job, etc. until after the next Encounter, though the Characters that leave due to his joining the group will do so immediately upon the death of the old Leader and so may not have Jobs assigned to them or their equipment changed prior to departing.

EXPERIENCE

All Characters in a group begin the Campaign with 0 Experience. During the course of the Campaign, they can earn Experience by doing the following during a game:

EXPERIENCE TABLE	
Action	**Experience Earned**
Taking a zombie Out of Action	+1
Taking a rival Group Member Out of Action	+3
Surviving a game (no being Out of Action at the end of a game)	+1D6
Fulfilling an Objective (starting an escape vehicle, rescuing a survivor, carrying a Supply Token, etc.)	+6

LEVEL UP

A newly recruited Character begins a Campaign at Level 0. During this post-game step, the models in a Group may spend Experience Points to advance in Level. Every time they do so they may choose to do one of two things:

1. To buy a roll on the Characteristics Increase table.
2. To buy a roll on one of the Skills Increase tables.

The cost of a Level on is shown on the table below. You will notice that as a model increases in power further rolls on the tables cost more and more. This will curb models becoming too powerful, too quickly and mean that as they begin to plateau, the increases in between Levels become greater.

LEVEL UP TABLE	
Level	**Cost in Experience**
Level 1	6 Experience
Level 2	12 Experience
Level 3	12 Experience
Level 4	18 Experience
Level 5	18 Experience
Level 6	18 Experience
Level 7	24 Experience
Level 8	24 Experience
Level 9	24 Experience
Level 10	30 Experience

Once Experience points are spent they are lost and a model must earn more to buy their next Level. Remember, a player can choose to roll on either the Characteristic or Skills tables as their advance, not both!

THE CHARACTERISTICS TABLE

When a model decides to buy a roll on the Characteristics Table roll 2D6 and check below:

CHARACTERISTIC TABLE	
2D6 Roll	**Characteristic Increase**
2	The model gains +1 to its Action Points
3	Roll again: On a roll of 1–3 the model gains +1 to their Close Quarters Combat. On a roll of 4–6 the model gains +1 to their Firearms
4	The model gains + 1 Strength
5	The model gains +1 Endurance
6	Roll again: On a 1–3 the model gains +1 Courage and on a 4–6 they gain +1 Intelligence.
7	Roll again: On a roll of 1–3 the model gains +1 to their Close Quarters Combat. On a roll of 4–6 the model gains +1 to their Firearms
8	The model gains +1 Strength
9	The model gains + 1 Endurance
10	Roll Again: Roll again: On a roll of 1–3 the model gains +1 to their Close Quarters Combat. On a roll of 4–6 the model gains +1 to their Firearms
11–12	The model gains + 1 Damage Capacity

A model can never increase a characteristic above six, apart from Action Points. If this occurs, roll again until the result is a different characteristic.

A model may spend up to three additional Experience points from its remaining pool to modify the roll on this table when they buy a level. If they do so, they may increase or decrease the roll by one for each Experience point spent in this way. This may be done to modify secondary rolls (if any) as well.

Record the increase on the Model's roster cards.

THE SKILLS TABLES

When a Character chooses to roll on a Skills Table you must first determine which areas of knowledge they have access to. Certain Characters will not have access to certain abilities. Refer to their unit cards for the skill types they are able to access.

When a Character rolls for a new skill, roll 1D6 and consult the appropriate table. If you roll a skill that they already know, re-roll until you get a result they do not already possess.

You may spend up to 3 additional Experience Points from the Character's remaining pool to modify the roll on these tables. If they do so, they may increase or decrease the roll by one for each Experience Point spent in this way.

ACADEMIC SKILLS TABLE	
D6 Roll	Skill
1	First Aid Training
2	Gear-Head
3	Engineer
4	Agriculturalist
5	Gunsmith
6	Scavenger

ATHLETIC SKILLS TABLE	
D6 Roll	Skill
1	Entry Man
2	Heavy Lifter
3	Free Runner
4	Sprinter
5	Situational Awareness
6	Stalker

CLOSE QUARTER COMBAT SKILLS TABLE	
D6 Roll	Skill
1	Crowd Control
2	Disarm
3	Headhunter
4	Subdue
5	Martial Arts
6	Dirty Fighter

LEADERSHIP SKILLS TABLE	
D6 Roll	Skill
1	Tactical Acumen
2	Inspirational Presence
3	Frontline Fighter
4	Tag-Team
5	Rallying Cry
6	Ambushers

SHOOTING SKILLS TABLE	
D6 Roll	Skill
1	Fire and Maneuver
2	Gunfighter
3	Sniper
4	Quick-load
5	Short Controlled Bursts
6	Double Tap

CHECKING SUPPLIES

After each Encounter the Characters will return to their Refuge, hopefully, laden down with supplies that can be used in to both fortify their home and better equip themselves for future Encounters with other Groups.

For each Supply Token successfully picked up by Characters and held or carried off the board when the game ended, roll 2D6 and consult the table below. A Group, that did not reach their Breaking Point, may also claim any untouched Supply Tokens left on the board if the hostile Group reached their Breaking Point, as they scour the area after their retreat for anything worth bringing back

SUPPLY TABLE					
2D6 Rolls	2-3	4-5	6-8	9-10	11-12
2	D6+6 Scavenge Points Minigun	D6+6 Scavenge Points Reflex Sight	D6+6 Scavenge Points Chainsaw	D6+6 Scavenge Points Combat Shotgun	D6+6 Scavenge Points Military Sniper Rifle
3	D6+6 Scavenge Points Military Assault Rifle	D6+6 Scavenge Points Silencer	D6+6 Scavenge Points	D6+6 Scavenge Points Hunting Crossbow	D6+6 Scavenge Points High-Power Rifle Scope
4	D6+6 Scavenge Points D3+1 Climbing Gear	D6+3 Scavenge Points Tactical Vest	D6+3 Scavenge Points Heavy Blade	D6+3 Scavenge Points Fire Bomb	D6+3 Scavenge Points D3+1 Booze
5	D6+3 Scavenge Points D3+1 Thrown Explosives	D6+3 Scavenge Points Surplus SMG	D6+3 Scavenge Points	D6+3 Scavenge Points Breach Loading Shotgun	D6+3 Scavenge Points D3+1 Medical Supplies
6	D6 Scavenge Points Surplus Assault Rifle	D6 Scavenge Points Semi-Automatic	D6 Scavenge Points Knife	D6 Scavenge Points Medical Supplies	D6 Scavenge Points D3 Semi-Automatics
7	D6 Scavenge Points Surplus SMG	D6 Scavenge Points Revolver	D6 Scavenge Points	D6 Scavenge Points Booze	D6 Scavenge Points Hunting Rifle
8	D6 Scavenge Points Military SMG	D6 Scavenge Points Magnum	D6 Scavenge Points Club	D6 Scavenge Points Climbing Gear	D6 Scavenge Points D3 Revolvers
9	D6+3 Scavenge Points D3+1 Medical Supplies	D6+3 Scavenge Points Thrown Explosive	D6+3 Scavenge Points	D6+3 Scavenge Points Hunting Bow	D6+3 Scavenge Points High-Power Rifle
10	D3+3 Scavenge Points D3+1 Silencers	D6+3 Scavenge Points Scope	D6+3 Scavenge Points Heavy Club	D6+3 Scavenge Points Fire Bomb	D6+3 Scavenge Points Hunting Rifle Scope
11	D6+6 Scavenge Points Squad Automatic Weapon	D6+6 Scavenge Points Noisemaker	D6+6 Scavenge Points	D6+6 Scavenge Points Pump Action Shotgun	D6+6 Scavenge Points D3 Hunting Rifles
12	D6+6 Scavenge Points Assault Armour	D6+6 Scavenge Points Military SMG	D6+6 Scavenge Points Riot Shield	D6+6 Scavenge Points Mod-Kit	D6+6 Scavenge Points D3 Mod Kits

Total all Scavenge Points and add them to the group's pool on the Group and Refuge card. Any equipment you find that you do not immediately equip to a Character you may also note down as stashed on the card.

At this point Characters may swap gear and re-arm themselves, moving equipment between themselves and the Group's stash.

REFUGE AND RECUPERATION

Once the Characters have carried their injured back home and inventoried what they've found, they will all disperse inside the Refuge to various necessary jobs or to recuperate from any injuries they have received during the course of the last game.

The Group's manpower available will need to be carefully considered as tasks are assigned. Do Characters set up watch to defend their injured friends or take the opportunity to reinforce their home by adding new Perks? No matter what they decide to do, the zombies are coming and will need to be driven off.

Finally, the Leader may attempt to recruit someone new into the Group. Only they may do this action.

RECOVERING FROM INJURIES

Characters who were taken Out of Action during a game will contribute very little back at the Refuge. Instead, they will need to be cared for by other Group members and will spend the time between their last encounter and the next being a drain on resources.

They may not be assigned any Jobs and will negatively affect the Group's chances during the subsequent Zombie Attack. Sometimes it's better to run than fight until the bitter end!

ASSIGNING JOBS

Characters who were not taken Out of Action during the previous game will all be assigned a Job. Everyone pulls their weight in the Group, in one way or another, as it is the only way they will survive.

A Character may:

GUARD

This Character spends their time patrolling the perimeter of the Refuge on the lookout for an approaching horde and killing lone zombies that stray too close. During the upcoming Zombie Attack they will give a bonus to defending the Refuge.

WORK

Some Perks of a Refuge allow for bonuses either immediately upon working them or for the next encounter. Some require a Character to actually work in the area. The Group will benefit from those Perks so long as someone is assigned to that Perk to generate them. One Character may work each Perk.

BUILD

Every Refuge will have empty spaces into which the Group can build new Perks. Each of these Perks will have a cost in resources – Scavenge Points – that must be paid. A Character must be assigned between games to actually construct or set up this new feature of the Refuge. Unless noted otherwise, Perks may only be built into a refuge once.

REFUGE PERKS TABLE	
Refuge Perks	**Scavenge Point Cost**
Armoury	20
Bunk Bed	20
Escape Vehicle	20
Fenced-Off Garden	15
Fences	20
Fortified Windows	20
Infirmary	25
Radio Room	15
Reinforced Doors	15
Solid Structure	30
Store Room	15
Watch Tower	20

RECRUIT

Only the Leader may be assigned this Job as only they will have the authority to negotiate or accept new people into the Refuge. If they are assigned to this Job, the Group may spend Scavenge Points to add one new Character following all the same rules and restrictions as when the Group was initially created and obeying the Maximum Group Size of the Refuge. That new Character will not participate in any Jobs themselves until after the next Encounter. They cannot be equipped out of the stash or have their starting weapons changed until after the next Encounter.

THE TALK

This Job requires two Characters: the Group's Leader and a Character with a different Keyword. Every Group has its outliers. Disagreements can cause strife but a good leader never stops trying to get the members of his Group to see things their way. Not following the plan can put everyone at risk. The Leader and other Character make an Opposed Intelligence Test. If the Leader is successful, the other Character's Keyword is immediately changed to the same as the Leaders.

ZOMBIE ATTACKS

Ongoing attacks from the undead are a fact of life in this new world. Attracted by simple movement and human activity, small roamers will attract larger groups until there are so many that their numbers become a problem and they begin to push into the Refuge. Preparing for the next assault is part of every day.

Injured Characters are a liability. Unable to fight and in the way, they hamper a Group's ability to defend the refuge. Characters actively patrolling and on Guard will mean the attack itself is easier to manage and prepare for.

After Injuries, Experience, Supplies, and Jobs are all resolved the zombies will attack.

Roll 2D6 and apply the following modifiers:

ZOMBIE ATTACKS TABLE	
Previous Encounter Results and other Effects	**Attack Roll Modifier**
For each Character Out of Action at the end of the previous Encounter	-1
For each Character on Guard	+1
The Refuge has the Fortified Windows Perk	+1

If the result is 2 or less the Group has been overwhelmed by the Zombie Attack and forced to abandon it in haste. If the final result is 3 or more, they have successfully defended the Refuge once again without incident.

LOSING YOUR REFUGE

Losing their home can mean a huge setback for the Group. They must immediately pick another Refuge which may **not** be of the same type as the one they currently occupy (this was the best option of its type in the area). In addition the Group is forced to abandon all their stashed equipment and weapons as they can take only what they can carry. The bank of Scavenge Points they currently have will remain unaffected. All Perks built into the Refuge are lost and will need to be rebuilt in the Group's new location. If the Group does not fit into the new location the Leader must make the unenviable decision of deciding who he will leave behind for the Zombies. Those Characters and all their equipment are considered dead and lost as they are slain by the undead. The Leader may not be picked to be left behind.

Finally, shuffle all the Group's Character cards face down and randomly select one. That character takes an additional Injury roll, as they are hurt either during the attack or during the escape later.

VOLUNTARILY LEAVING YOUR REFUGE

Sometimes a Group just needs more space. A Group may voluntarily abandon their current Refuge for a new one, provided they successfully defend it from a Zombie Attack. They still lose all built in Perks they have accumulated but in this case as the move is planned, they may transport all their stashed weapons and equipment to the new location as well as their accumulated Scavenge Points. Just like when fleeing from a Zombie Attack, they may not move into the same **type** of Refuge. They must also decide if the Group needs to abandon any Characters who will not fit. The Leader must always be selected to go to the new Refuge as it is they who are making the decision.

ENCOUNTERS

The most common type of Encounter between rival Groups of survivors in *Last Days* is when two groups of scavengers encounter each other while searching for supplies outside their respective Refuges. These rivalries soon escalate. As the Groups become aware of the other hostile survivors in the area, they will come into greater conflict and launch both planned and spontaneous attacks of opportunity.

For your first game of *Last Days* you should play the Encounter 5: Scavengers. This Encounter focuses on the core mechanics of retrieving resources while fending off enemy characters and is perfect for learning the game.

When setting up an Encounter for *Last Days* after your first, roll 1D6 and consult the table below.

ENCOUNTERS TABLE	
1D6 Roll	**Encounter**
1	Bushwhack
2	Home Defense
3	Massacre Site
4	Rescue
5	Scavengers
6	The Escape

ENCOUNTER 1: BUSHWHACK

There is no code of conduct when you are fighting for survival in the zombie apocalypse. Catching a portion of your enemies off-guard and unaware means you may be able to quickly defeat them and make off with whatever they have found. Robbery is far easier than real work.

SET UP

Instead of the usual deployment method, one Group will be the attackers and the other will be defending. If one Group is led by a Selfish Leader, they will automatically be the attacker unless the defender is also Selfish. In all other cases, Roll-Off to see who attacks and who defends.

Set up terrain as normal but leave the center of the board open except for small scatter terrain. This is where the defenders have taken a break during their Scavenging. The defenders may deploy up to three Characters, one of whom must be the Leader, within 6" of the center of the board. Mark each one as carrying a Supply Token.

The attacker may deploy up to six Characters, including their Leader, after this is done. Any others in the Group are left behind at their refuge as only a small force would be able to sneak up on the defenders. These Characters may be deployed anywhere within 3" of any board edge.

Once both sides are deployed, the players should Roll-Off and place 3 zombies anywhere on the board, but not within 6" of a board edge or Characters from either Group.

SPECIAL RULES

During the Menace Phase, when rolling for Noise Tokens, any time a zombie would be summoned to the table by Tokens from either side, the defender may instead place one Group member onto the board that was not deployed at the beginning of the Encounter. The sound of battle alerts them to the danger and sends them rushing to their friends aid. They will activate as normal during the Action Phase. Once all the defender's Characters arrive, zombies will appear as normal.

ENDING THE GAME

The Encounter will end when all Supply Tokens have left the table or one, or both, Groups reach their Breaking Point.

ENCOUNTER 2: HOME DEFENSE

Stumbling upon the Refuge of another group can result in all-out battle. The defenders home is stockpiled with resources, equipment, weapons, and may even be better equipped than the attacking Group's own. The Encounter will be brutal, as the Group fighting for their home is making a final stand and will not give up their Refuge without a fight. Whether to raid for supplies or to take over the Refuge itself, the attackers will not have an easy go of it.

SET UP

Roll-Off to determine which Group is the attacker and which is the defender. The defender should set up an appropriate building to represent their Refuge. It should have at least two doors (see the rules for doors, page 35), four windows, and a minimum footprint of 6"x6". In the case of the Mall, imagine it is a section of a larger structure, or perhaps an outdoor shopping center. This scenario is a great opportunity to add terrain features to your collection to appropriately represent the defenders home. Set up the rest of the terrain as normal.

The players Roll-Off and take turns deploying 3 Supply Tokens inside the Refuge and 2 more outside the Refuge but still within 4" of it.

The Defending group must deploy their Characters within 4" of the Refuge. The attackers then deploy their Characters within 3" of any of the four table edges.

Finally, deploy 3 zombies anywhere on the board but not within 6" of any Character, or within the Refuge.

SPECIAL RULES

The defenders have nowhere to go and will fight to the last. They do not make Breaking Point Tests during this Encounter. As they are already at their Refuge, they may not carry Supply Tokens off the board.

ENDING THE GAME

The Encounter ends when all the of the Supply Tokens have left the table, the attackers reach their Breaking Point, or all of the defenders are Out of Action.

ENCOUNTER 3: MASSACRE SITE

Millions of tiny, tragic stories unfolded during the fall of civilization. Stumbling upon these vignettes or even more recent survivors that have finally fallen to the zombies can often result in valuable supplies. People ran for less populated areas often supplied and stocked with all kinds of valuable equipment. When one of these sites is discovered, Groups will fight savagely to secure them.

SET UP

Set up the terrain as normal. To make the Encounter more thematic, you could place wrecked vehicles or some other evidence of a previous fight in the center of the board. After both Groups are deployed, the players should Roll-Off and take it in turns deploying 5 zombies anywhere within 8" of the center point of the table. These represent the victims who were massacred by zombies. Each zombie carries a single Supply Token, representing the equipment they carried when they died.

SPECIAL RULES

Remember that the zombies are carrying Supply Tokens and will be effected by the Heavy special rule.

ENDING THE GAME

The Encounter ends when all of the Supply Tokens have left the table or one, or both, Groups reach their Breaking Point.

ENCOUNTER 4: RESCUE

With life being as brutal and short as it is in this new world, Leaders will often go to great lengths to save the members of their Group. Whether one of the Characters has found themselves at the mercy of a hostile Group or the attackers have come across a wandering survivor being held at the mercy of the defenders, a rescue is being mounted.

SET UP

Set up terrain for the Encounter as normal and Roll-Off to place 3 Supply Tokens within 8" of the center of the table. Unless one Group has Characters who were captured in the previous Encounter, rRoll-Off to determine who the attacker and defender is. If both players have captured Characters, Roll-Off to determine who is mounting the first Rescue Encounter.

Place an appropriate model to represent the Captive in the center of the board, or the model(s) of any Captured Characters. The defender may deploy up to three Characters, including the Leader, within 6" of the Captive(s). The attackers may deploy up to six Characters, including their Leader, within 3" of any of the table edges. Finally, the players Roll-Off and deploy 3 zombies anywhere on the table, but not within 6" of any Character.

SPECIAL RULES

During the Menace Phase, when rolling for Noise Tokens, any time a zombie would be summoned to the table by tokens from either side, the defender may instead place one Group member that was not deployed at the beginning of the Encounter as the sound of battle alerts them to the danger and sends them rushing to their friends aid. They will activate as normal during the Action Phase. Once all the defender's Characters arrive, zombies will appear as normal.

Each Captive can be interacted with exactly like a Supply Token, as they are incapacitated and need assistance.

ENDING THE GAME

The Encounter ends when all of the Supply Tokens and Captives have left the table or one, or both, Groups reach their Breaking Point.

If the attackers retrieve a Captive Character, they re-join their friends with their weapons and equipment intact. If the defenders retrieve a Captive, they will interrogate and either kill or leave them for the zombies and take all their weapons and equipment.

If either side retrieves a Captive that is not a Character that Group may add a single unarmed Survivor (Neutral) to their Group, provided there is room to do so in their Refuge.

ENCOUNTER 5: SCAVENGERS

Getting supplies back to your Refuge in preparation for the next attack and equipping the Group with better weapons and equipment is a vital and daily task the Characters will face. Venturing out is never easy, and when you make contact with other such groups of runners it can often end in violence.

SET UP

Set up Terrain for the Encounter as normal and place Supply Tokens in the usual way. After both Groups are deployed, the players should Roll-Off and take it in turns deploying 3 zombies anywhere within 6" of the center line of the table. This represents the roaming undead already on the board.

SPECIAL RULES

None.

ENDING THE GAME

The Encounter ends when all of the Supply Tokens have left the table or one, or both, Groups reach their Breaking Point.

(OPTIONAL) ENDING THE CAMPAIGN

While it can be immensely satisfying to create a climactic Encounter to end your Campaign of *Last Days*, the reality is that Groups are stockpiling resources to survive. In many areas this means preparing for seasonal weather changes that can be deadly in a world without electricity or other resources the modern world takes for granted.

If this Optional rule is used, then the first Group in the Campaign to fully upgrade all Empty Spaces in their Refuge and reach their Maximum Group size while collecting 300 unspent Scavenge Points in their stash will be considered to have stripped the area of resources and be the Group that will survive the upcoming changing of the seasons. The grim fates of the other Groups remain unknown.

ENCOUNTER 6: THE ESCAPE

A massive horde of zombies is descending on the area and two rival Groups find themselves directly in its path. There are far too many to fight and both sides are desperately searching for a vehicle large enough to carry them out of danger.

SET UP

Place an appropriate model to represent the vehicle that both Groups have identified as able to save them from horde, in the center of the table. Set up terrain around the vehicle for the Encounter as normal and place Supply Tokens in the usual way. After both Groups are deployed, the players should Roll-Off and take it in turns deploying 3 zombies anywhere within 6" of the center line of the table to represent the roaming undead already on the board.

SPECIAL RULES

The escape vehicle needs to be repaired so that it may start before it can be used to escape from the horde. A Character must use an Interact action and pass an Intelligence/15 Test in order to start the vehicle and get away. Each subsequent Interact action on the vehicle gives a cumulative +1 bonus to the roll for Characters from either Group, as the vehicle is continually repaired.

As the horde is descending upon the area, whenever a zombie would be summoned to the Encounter place two zombies instead of just one. As both Groups are surrounded, neither one needs test for their Breaking Point during this Encounter as the vehicle represents the best chance of escape.

ENDING THE GAME

The Encounter ends when a Character from either Group succeeds in starting the vehicle or one side's Characters are all Out of Action. In that case, the Group with active Characters is considered to have secured the Escape Vehicle.

At the end of the Encounter, the Group that escaped may select a single Character to work on the vehicle they secured. If they can pass an Intelligence/8 Test, they may add an Escape Vehicle Perk to their Refuge, if they do not already have one. They repair the damage caused by their flight from the Horde.

CREATING YOUR APOCALYPSE

This rulebook intentionally avoids trying to set the scene or build a world for *Last Days: Zombie Apocalypse*. The reason for that is simple; it's set in **your** world.

One of the most satisfying experiences you can have is playing out the zombie zpocalypse in **your** town or City. Create terrain to represent your locale and even tailor your Refuges to be local landmarks. While these rules can be easily used to set your apocalypse anywhere, it can be a lot of fun to 'go with what you know'.

Here are some notes on resources:

MODELS

Creating a collection of models to play out *Last Days* can allow you to pull models from all kinds of different ranges. There are a ton of board games and independent companies producing appropriate models. Hasslefree Miniatures are featured throughout this book but there are numerous other companies out there to choose from as well as lots of great Board Game figures that could be used as well.

TERRAIN

Last Days can be set anywhere in the world, so how you collect terrain for your games is up to you. That being said, O-Scale model railroad buildings can be a great source for getting started and there are more and more MDF terrain kits available every year, allowing you to make your gaming table just how you like.

VEHICLES

1:43 scale die-cast vehicles make up the bulk of what is seen in the photography in this rulebook. They can come from anywhere, but keeping a model of the appropriate scale in your coat pocked means when you come across vehicles at souvenir shops, the local pharmacy, or the airport allows you to have something with which to eyeball whether or not it looks like the right size.

Rather than try to cover everything in this section you can join the discussion in the official Facebook group for *Last Days* where you will be able to see tons of inspiring model and terrain collections and get to work on your own with the advice of other talented hobbyists.

ACKNOWLEDGEMENTS AND THANKS

It would be impossible to thank everyone who has influenced me over the years in this industry, but if we have spent time together working in this strange wonderful business of toy soldiers you know who you are. This book is the result of hundreds of quiet moments, conversations, and adventures with those talented people I have been lucky enough to know. I do want to take a moment to thank my wife ,Cassie, and two incredible kids, Catena and Cash, for the endless support and joy they bring me as well as my Mum, Dad, and Sister for all of their encouragement and love.

MINIATURE PAINTING

Ash Barker

ART

Arthur Asa

TERRAIN MODELLING AND PAINTING

Ash Barker, Adam Rogers, Austin Thompson, Joe Borawski,

PHOTOGRAPHY

Ash Barker

MINIATURES

Hasslefree Miniatures, RAFM, Studio Miniatures, Armorcast

BUILDING KITS

Death Ray Designs, Black Site Studios, MC Studios, Demo's Laser Cut Designs

GAMING MATS

Urban Matz, GameMat.eu

Thanks!

CHARACTER AND REFUGE CARDS

CHARACTER ROSTER

Name									
Characteristics	AP	CQC	FA	S	E	DC	C	I	
Character Type				Keyword					
Equipment									
Special Rules									
Skills									
Notes									
Level				Experience					

Name									
Characteristics	AP	CQC	FA	S	E	DC	C	I	
Character Type				Keyword					
Equipment									
Special Rules									
Skills									
Notes									
Level				Experience					

Name									
Characteristics	AP	CQC	FA	S	E	DC	C	I	
Character Type				Keyword					
Equipment									
Special Rules									
Skills									
Notes									
Level				Experience					

Name									
Characteristics	AP	CQC	FA	S	E	DC	C	I	
Character Type				Keyword					
Equipment									
Special Rules									
Skills									
Notes									
Level				Experience					

Name									
Characteristics	AP	CQC	FA	S	E	DC	C	I	
Character Type				Keyword					
Equipment									
Special Rules									
Skills									
Notes									
Level				Experience					

Name									
Characteristics	AP	CQC	FA	S	E	DC	C	I	
Character Type				Keyword					
Equipment									
Special Rules									
Skills									
Notes									
Level				Experience					

GROUP AND REFUGE

GROUP AND REFUGE			
Refuge Type		Empty Spaces	
Maximum Group Size		Scavenge Points	

BUILT-IN PERKS	

PERKS	

NOTES AND STASHED EQUIPMENT

GROUP MEMBERS

YA

Last Days Zombie apo
01/31/2022